GW01057608

VAMPIRE'S SHADE

**VIVIENNE
NEAS**
BLUE SHELF BOOKSTORE

No part of this book may be reproduced, or stored in a retrieval system, or transmitted in any form or by any means, electronic, mechanical, photocopying, recording or otherwise, without express written permission of the publisher.

Published by BlueShelfBookstore

www.blueshelfbookstore.com

Vampire's Shade
© 2015 BlueShelfBookstore
All rights reserved

Get even better value for money when you purchase the Vampire's Shade Discounted Box Set for $7.99, instead of paying a total of $12 when you buy each book separately. Just type **"Vampire's Shade Discounted Box Set"** *on the Store Search Bar.*

Chapter 1

I backed the vampire into an alley, my knife out with the sharp end low and threatening. The silver gleamed in the almost-darkness of the alley, a reminder to me and my victim that it had silver in it. A black chain was looped over my shoulder, weighing me down, but I trained like this. I could deal. I was just trying to scare the vampire with my knife. The short silver blade wasn't good for a kill, not for a vampire. It would do in a pinch, the silver burned their flesh – not enough but a little – and I could work it over if I wanted to, but I would get my hands dirty, and I preferred to stake them.

Or blow their heads off. I had yet to see a vampire that could bounce back from that one.

The vampire tried to dodge me and escape, but I had the upper hand. I knew about the vampire's speed. It had underestimated mine. I was in front of it before it reached me.

It skidded to halt, gaping at me. In a life-and-death fight there wasn't a lot of time for questions. You got to choose – answers or life. The vampire had made the wrong choice. I let the chain slip off my shoulder and swung it around, sheathing the knife with my free hand. I flicked the chain at the vampire. It twisted around its wrist and the clip snapped shut around itself. This baby was going nowhere.

Blue and red lights suddenly danced on the street at the alley entrance, and we both froze. The battle between us was one thing, but neither of us wanted the police involved. I didn't, because my work had a lot of moral pitfalls. The vampire didn't because in a case where a vampire man and human woman were in an alley together, chances were the police would take the human's side. Besides that there was also the small technicality that I wasn't exactly human, and I supposedly didn't exist.

When the car had driven past and the silence of night fell around us again, I looked at my victim and smiled.

I stepped closer to the vampire, looping the chain as I came closer until my body was almost right up against the vampire's. It squirmed and tried to fight, but it had been a long run to get here, and I was fitter. The vampire squeezed its eyes shut and I felt a hum emanating from it. The vamp faded so I could see the brick wall right through its chest, but the metal I'd wrapped around its wrist stopped it from dematerializing completely, and when it stopped trying to, the humming stopped, too. I was going to win this one, and it knew.

I flipped my hair over my shoulder to get it out of the way. In the tussle I'd lost the hairband that kept the black mass of hair out of my face. I killed for a living, and my biggest stumbling block was keeping my long hair out of the way.

Beauty was a bitch.

I wasn't going to cut it. It hung halfway down my back, thick and healthy. I may not have been your standard home-maker kind of woman, but my looks were just as deadly as my skill. And I had a lot of skill.

I wrapped the chain around the other wrist, too, and tightened it, pulling its hands up with one hand. With the other I placed a silver stake under the vampire's ribs, and wrapped my fingers tightly around the smooth finish, fingering the pattern I'd carved out around its edge. I carried a lot of heat, I had a gun in the holster under my jacket and another tucked into my waistband at the small of my back. But guns didn't work on vampires. The fast-healing action was a pain in the ass when it came to self-defense or hit-jobs.

The vampire's eyes were wild, wide, rolling around in their sockets. The split-second before death was never pretty. A thick black mist surrounded us, choking me, making it hard to breathe.

I gritted my teeth and ignored it. It was almost like poison, a last attempt at life, like an octopus's ink, but I was immune. Never underestimate your enemies.

Aspen's eyes flashed in front of me, dull and lifeless. Her body bent at an impossible angle. The room with the furniture upside down and out of place like a nightmare version of our home. Bloody fangs dripping menace. A fire inside me threatened to consume me and I leaned against the stake, pushing into flesh, forcing my way into the vampire's heart. Killing the memories.

The vampire focused on me, questioning, eyes draining of life already, and a flicker of recognition passed across its face. Fast reflexes, stronger than human women, immune to the mist. It knew what I was. The pain of betrayal was the last emotion before its face went slack, its eyes rolled back, and the body slumped forward. Yeah, this one was going to haunt me. Great start to my week.

I swallowed and gasped for air. The thick stench clung to my clothes even after the mist had gone and I couldn't shake the feeling of darkness and death clawing at my ankles. I shuddered. Guilt was about as ugly as death itself.

I pushed the dead vampire off me, letting the body crumple to the ground. I wiped the stake clean on my black leather pants, and zipped my jacket up half-way to conceal the gun. The silver line of dawn was on the horizon, bleeding into the inky night air, announcing Tuesday morning. The rising sun would take care of everything else, the blood, the body. The darkness I just couldn't seem to get away from.

I turned and walked away, but stopped before I turned out of the alley. I bit my cheek, and turned back. I had to frisk the damn thing. This part I hated the most. Nothing as bad as playing with the dead when you were the reason they were dead in the first place.

I ignored the seed of guilt that throbbed deep down. I tried to shake the image of the vampire's face when it realized what I was.

I may have been a half-breed, at least fifty percent one of them, but genetics was as far as it went. My loyalty lay with humans.

My phone chirped in my pocket and I answered it, clamping it against my shoulder with my cheek. Small miracle I hadn't lost it in the fight. That wouldn't have been the first time. Hi-tech was worth nothing if it fell out of my pocket.

"Are you coming in before dawn?" Ruben's voice was clipped.

"I'm on my way to the office now."

"Cutting it a bit close, aren't you Adele?"

"I don't tell you how to do your job, Ruben. Let me do mine." My boss was a hard-ass idiot that believed he knew everything there was to know about night-creatures, even though he never set foot outside his office until sunrise. He knew what the dangers were, and he wasn't going to take the fall. He trusted everyone about the same amount, which was not at all. I liked him best when he was riled up and it was my fault.

"Just get in here to do the paper-work. I don't want any mistakes. That damn Clemens woman was here again tonight, and I don't want a story about you in the news."

"Since when do journalists do nighttime visits?"

"Since you don't have the day shift. I don't want to start my week like this, Adele."

Like it was my fault.

Ruben hung up the phone and I shuddered in the silence it left behind. There weren't a lot of people that believed in half-breeds, and those that did wished us dead. I shook off the feeling of foreboding that had come with the phone call, and headed downtown.

I was a vampire slayer for a living. I was good at what I did and Ruben paid me well for it. It was quick work even though it wasn't always easy. And it wasn't just the physical side that provided a problem. But every job had its emotional downside. Some people needed TV-time to wind down after the daily grind. I probably needed therapy.

I worked for a thickset man in a dirty world. Ruben Cross was about as human as he came, but his scent disgusted me. I could smell his blood and it was laced with alcohol most of the time. He was dead set against vampires, because of religion as much as racism. On the outside his company looked like a standard accounting firm. His after-hour advertising happened among chosen individuals, a private affair among people that heard of us by word-of-mouth in whispers around corners and only a few knew about what we did when night fell.

We weren't exactly on the radar, and I liked it that way. My entire existence was under the radar. The unlicensed killing meant I never had to own up to anything, and we didn't speak of a job once it was done. Vampires didn't quite fall under any constitution yet. They were seen as part of society now, but those that didn't fear them shunned them, and everyone had a healthy dose of discrimination. Human rights got a little blurry when they weren't human, but the fewer questions asked, the better.

Vampires had a strange hierarchy, and the ones we ended up taking out were the mundane vampires, the young ones, the ones that didn't mean anything in the vampire world. The jobs were usually ordered by humans. The vampires that meant something, the powerful ones at the top of their own food chain, those we left alone. They never had quarrels with humans and we never ran into real killers. Still, when a cop found a body in the street, supernatural creature or not, it was going to attract attention.

The common consensus was that humans and vampires couldn't breed. Half-breeds were rumors, and as far as most people were concerned Aspen and I couldn't even exist. Ruben knew what I was, but he kept me on because as a half-breed I had the uncanny ability to pull off looking completely human. I also had vampire characteristics which gave me an advantage above the human slayers. It upped my chances of tricking the beasts and getting them down before it turned into a moral issue.

Betraying our own was a big deal, but I had a hatred for vampires that almost equaled Ruben's own. Why did I hate them? He had his reasons, I had mine. I had a strict don't ask don't tell policy.

So far, it's worked for me.

When I stepped into the lobby of the office building where Ruben holed up, Carl was just coming down the stairs. He was a lot of man, muscle that made his shirt stretch tight over his arms and thighs that threatened to pop out of his pants. Muscles were no good when they were only for show. If it came down to a life or death fight I could have taken him easy. Muscle is worth nothing against a gun.

"Oh, you're here too," he said. We didn't often rub shoulders, not since he'd taken me out on his first kill so I could learn the ropes. He was always sarcastic about my job, something a woman wouldn't be able to do. But we both knew it was about the fact that within in a week I'd been better at his job than he was.

When I looked at him closely I saw the toll the last couple of years had taken on him. He had new wrinkles, he didn't look like the young, strapping lad that had taken me under his wing anymore. He looked worn. I wondered if the same counted for me. It was hard to stay in this kind of line and look fresh at the end of the day.

"Just doing the final rounds, Carl," I said. "I don't feel like getting into a brawl tonight."

"You're in the wrong line for that," he pointed out. I shrugged. Carl was just a human. I didn't know how he managed to do his job – the first night I'd seen him he'd been quick and that had been his only asset. Still, Ruben kept him on so maybe he had something going for him. Maybe he charmed them to death. With his chiseled jaw and jet black hair he could get any woman to look twice. Maybe his icy eyes did the trick to hypnotize the vampires into believing they shouldn't run.

I passed him and he tipped his shoulder so it knocked me in the arm. In a world where we're vampire slayers there are no courtesies for women. I jabbed my elbow back faster than he could blink and caught him in the kidney. He made a strangled sound.

"You better watch your back, Adele. Sometimes humans can hold grudges too."

"If you're talking about yourself I'm not exactly going to lose sleep over it. But thanks for the warning."

He snorted and walked out into the silvery dawn. Carl wasn't a bad guy all round, I just didn't like him. There was a time when we got along, but he'd gotten cocky about his kills and somewhere along the lines he'd picked up that I was a half-breed. That made all the difference, usually. He didn't see me as an equal anymore. Good thing I never really cared. I was good at working alone, and his smoldering looks might have worked on other females, but I didn't have time for dating.

"That's what I'm talking about," Ruben said when I walked into his office and dropped the ID card and keys I'd taken off the vampire on his desk. His salt-and-pepper hair looked like he'd spent a night sticking his hands into it, and he wore a jersey over his shirt that I would bet hid the fact that it was creased. The smell of whiskey hung in the air, lacing the day-old smell of his cologne, and I crinkled my nose. He picked up the ID and looked at the photo. He nodded, satisfied. "It took Carl a week and he still couldn't put this one down. And you do it as a quickie on the side."

"Not my fault you're not delegating right, Ruben," I said. "I told you this one wasn't going to go down easy. Some of them you have to get hot and heavy with."

"Nothing as hot as a vampire slayer willing to get personal." He shook his head, his amber eyes were bright despite the fact that he looked like he could do with a year of sleep. "I wish there were more people like you on my team. Carl is good but he's not you, and I've already got your quota filled." He leaned on his desk and intertwined his own fingers. "About this journalist. You need to watch your back. She's not letting this one go."

"Nothing I can't handle. You know that."

He stretched his arms up and his jersey pulled taut over the expanse of his body. Under the desk I noticed he was wearing slippers. I guess if I were stuck in this office all night I would do something to get comfortable too.

"You're not immortal, Adele. If anyone finds out what you are, what you're doing is only going to count against you."

"I'm doing what most humans are too scared to."

"And you're an abomination..."

I turned and walk out of the office before he could finish his sentence. He didn't reserve the right to hire a killer *and* lecture her. I didn't want to hear how wrong I was. He had to stay clear; I beat myself up enough without him joining in. "You make sure you're back here by sundown," Ruben called after me. I didn't bother to answer.

Being a half breed meant there were some rules that didn't apply. My human genes won out more often than not. Things like the fact that I had a perfect set of blunt teeth – no fangs – and I didn't need blood to survive, even though I could smell it and sometimes it called out to me. The sun was uncomfortable, but it wasn't going to turn me into ash.

Ruben knew it, but we worked on a schedule that stretched from sunset to sunrise. He had me working all night as it was. I wasn't going to give him a chance to put me on double duty. Daylight was a better time to hunt vampires, if you could find where they holed up. But I had a thing about killing something helpless. Even if it was a vampire. I'd seen enough of that in my life to know that something deserved a fighting chance, at least. I refused to slay in daytime. Personal policy. Besides, everyone needed downtime, and that included me.

I found my motorcycle three blocks in the opposite direction of my home, on the outskirts of Westham's Business District where I'd abandoned it when the vampire had hopped a fence my motorcycle couldn't. I was attracted to raw power, and the MV Augusta M4CC was just that. It had a black body with smooth curves and it was an orgasm on wheels.

Where did a civilian like me with a slightly-above-average income get her hands on something as rare as an Augusta? Vampires have resources, and I happened to kill the right one. Who would have thought my job had perks.

The bike purred underneath me and the wind wrapped around my body as I raced down the street. The speed gave me the illusion that I was actually escaping for a change. I preferred it to walking, not just because it was a hot piece of metal, but because the neighborhood wasn't a great one and I was a girl that was said to get attention. Not that I had any trouble. The last man that ran his hand up my thigh when I'd politely asked him to back off was still trying to figure out which way was up. Still, my ride was a reward, and after a night of kills I wasn't in the mood to play nice.

I turned into my street. It was another couple of blocks to my apartment building, and shadows lurked in between trash cans and narrow alleys. I twisted the throttle and ate up the distance. It wasn't that I didn't like the place. It was just that the threatening shadows reminded me of what could hide in them. Once you opened yourself up to the creepy crawlies of the night, you never really escaped them again. I wanted to be off duty at some point. I didn't like killing after hours and Ruben wasn't going to pay me overtime.

A sharp scent flowed in through the air vents in my helmet and pulled my head to the right. I slowed down the bike, stopped, and backed up with my toes on the tarmac until I almost felt the smell inside of me. I fought the urge, but it drew me. Being a half-breed meant blood could call out to me, and I wasn't as immune to it as I liked. It was a weakness in the field I didn't like to acknowledge.

I knew the smell of vampire, and it was my downfall that I couldn't ignore the call if it was on the right frequency. This one had something else to it too, though. Something I couldn't quite place. The draw was stronger than usual.

I switched off the bike and got off, pulling my helmet off and leaving it hanging on the handle. My hair fell into my face and I shook my head irritably and followed my nose. It wasn't the safest place to leave a bike unattended, but I didn't plan on staying very long. I looked up and down the street but I was alone. In all black clothing I was camouflaged for night time, but with the rising sun I stuck out against the silvery color of morning.

The scent pulled me and I sniffed it out like a bloodhound. I walked into an alley that had walls reaching three stories up on either side, and it ran into a dead end at the back, a chain link fence that looked onto a dumpster. My nose prickled with the pungent smell. It was sour and it spelled out trouble.

When I moved the trash cans around the fence at the back where the scent hung heavy in the air, a pale hand fell onto my foot, and I jumped. I wasn't nervous as a rule, but this could be a trap as much as anything else.

I reached behind my back and gripped the SIG Sauer P226. I'd left my stake with the bike and the only other gun that I still had silver bullets for was the Beretta at home. It was costly to be cocky. This gun wouldn't do much damage to a vampire who could heal at will and had the force of fury behind him, but it would slow it down long enough for me to get away. I wished I had more bullets for my Smith & Wesson. I was fresh out of shot. The 500 packed a punch that could kill a large animal. I still had to meet a vampire that could hold onto its head after a good aim. The gap between life and death was only a hairline crack when you stared down the right barrel.

The hand on my foot was limp. I pointed my gun, and trailed it up a well-shaped arm. On the other end of it I found a male vampire. The skin was tight over its skull and almost translucent in its neck. It was unconscious, it's cheeks sunken and dark circles around its closed eyes. Its skin wasn't as pale as some of the older vampires I'd seen despite the dull, almost colorless appearance of its hair that made it look washed out, and it had fresh puncture marks at the base of its neck. A couple of them, with the skin bruised around the bites.

This vampire was freshly turned, and left out here in the ally to die. Why? I looked around, preparing for company, but the atmosphere around us was empty. I couldn't smell anyone. A vampire didn't become a vampire by accident. It took a lot of work – a person had to be held for a number of days and drank from at regular intervals until there was nothing left to give. Death by absolute blood loss turned it, when the body had to mutate to survive. Death by consumption. I smiled at my own joke.

Generally vampires just bred to make more vampires. But humans were turned sometimes, too. Usually with good reason, but it often remained a mystery.

After all that trouble to recruit, why would it be left here to die at sunrise? Unless it had escaped. I considered getting my stake. I should have killed it right there. One vampire less to deal with when the time came. But when I looked at its face, I couldn't do it. My values were twisted, but I had a set of rules I tried to live by. Helplessness tugged at my heartstrings, and I couldn't just turn my face away and shoot point-blank. The vampire had dirty-blond hair and flawless skin, like porcelain. Vampires were slimmer than people, tall and skinny, but even so it must have worked out in its past life. Still, all that muscle was no good when it was unconscious. It would be wrong to kill it.

I grabbed it by the ankles and dragged it down the alley towards the street. The sun was heading this way soon, and even the first rays of dawn were fatal for a pure-blood. It was heavier than it looked, and I was stronger than most girls with my supernatural gifts. Its arms flipped up and the shirt rode up. The concrete was going to leave a hell of a graze, but if it survived it would be healed up in no time. Possibly even before it woke up, if it ever did.

I worked my way across the street, keeping an eye out for danger. The street was deserted. When I got to the other side I kicked a closed garage door. It lifted enough on its hinges for me to work with. I worked my fingers underneath and it rolled to the top with a groan. No one had lived here for years. The vampire would be safe, and ready to dematerialize by sun down if another predator didn't sniff it out first.

I shoved the body into the cold garage and slammed the door shut again without looking at it, dusting my hands on my pants. When I walked away I knew I was going to regret saving the vamp, but I would get it another time. I didn't like going after vampires who hadn't done anything wrong, even though they deserved it just as much.

Chapter 2

In my apartment I double-locked the front door and checked the windows. It was a habit to make sure I was alone in the house. My windows were barred but that was enough metal for me. As much as I didn't want them to materialize into my house, I also wanted them to be able to dematerialize out of it when it came down to it.

My place was in a bad part of town. I earned enough for something better, but the illusion of safety made me nauseous. I wanted to be on guard because I had to. I couldn't become comfortable. It was in a well-off neighborhood, a lovely family home, where I'd lost my mother and nearly my sister. No thank you, I preferred to slum it.

I stripped my weapons and put them in the gun safe at the bottom of my cupboard. I peeled off the holster and thigh sheath and hung them up next to my leather jacket.

I showered. I had to get the acidic smell of that mist off me, and get rid of any blood that might have gotten on my skin. I killed for a living, but the idea of blood made me sick.

The face looking back at me in the mirror was haunted. My black hair framed a too-white face. I had the classic vampire complexion. My face was smooth and flawless, but a long scar ran from my jaw down my neck and ended at the base of my collar bone. I traced it with my finger.

By the time the sun fell into my bedroom window I was ready to leave again. My hair was dry and tied up in a bun, and I wore grey slacks and an aqua shirt. The blue made my eyes stand out. In my leathers they looked like ice. Dressed like a normal person there was some depth to them. I didn't take my bike, instead I took the bus to the other side of Westham, where there were flower boxes under the windows and a reminder that nocturnal life didn't dominate.

Zelda opened the door. She was the live-in nurse that helped Aspen. Her white uniform strained against her solid frame and her hair was pulled back against her head with no imagination. One thing I could say about Zelda was that she was consistent.

"Adele," she said, smiling when she saw me like it was a surprise, even though no one else ever called this early. "How are you?"

"Fine," I answered, but Zelda shook her head.

"You should sleep more."

I shrugged. I would if I could.

"Go on through to the kitchen," she said. "She's waiting for you."

When I walked into the kitchen the buttery roll-up blinds were drawn against the sun. Aspen didn't need the sun to drain the little bit of energy she had. She had more vampire in her than I did, and her skin didn't like the touch of sun very much. Aspen sat at the counter they lowered for her wheelchair.

"There you are," she said when she saw me, and smiled. Her pearly white fangs showed, and the combination with her dainty face, ghostly white skin and cascading honey curls made her look like she stepped out of a fantasy novel. My sister and I were total opposites. I had black hair and blue eyes. She had blond hair and hazel eyes. She was the lucky one that had our mother stare back at her when she looked in the mirror, despite her fangs which our human mother hadn't had. I was saddled up with the looks of my dead-beat father minus the teeth, but I didn't want to be reminded of him every day. I was pretty, but looks could kill in a lot of different ways.

"How are you doing?" I asked, bending down to kiss her on the head. I couldn't help but notice her legs when I did. Thin and frail from years' of lack of use. When she reached across the counter for her orange juice, her arm was thin and bony.

"You've lost weight again," I said, frowning. "If you keep at it, one day there will be nothing left of you." I sat down on a chair that always stood there for me, and took a piece of toast.

"Already only half left," she said and laughed. Her laugh danced around the kitchen like chimes, but I didn't join in. I didn't think her joke was funny. Her laughter faded when she saw my lack of humor, but the golden flecks in her eyes held onto the joke.

"Stop fussing over me, tell me about your night. Did you catch any bad ones?"

I shrugged and bit off a piece of toast. I was hazy about what I did when it came down to family. To Aspen I was the hero, the one that had gotten out unscathed and now devoted my life to fighting crime, putting bad guys behind bars. I wasn't going to talk about gruesome deaths to my handicapped sister, explaining that if the police got a hold of me, I was probably the one that would end up behind bars. It was bad enough that she had to sit in a wheelchair all her life. She didn't have to know the gory details of how I tried to make up for my failure to protect her.

"You don't have to keep coming around after your shift, you know," Aspen said when I wouldn't answer her. "I know you're tired. You always insist on the graveyard shift."

Graveyard shift. Huh. The irony.

"And what am I going to do for a social life then?" I asked, pulling a face. I didn't know a lot of people besides Joel, my weapons specialist. The ones I met I usually ended up killing.

"You should get yourself a boyfriend, it would be good for you to have someone take care of you for a change. I never can."

Her words hit me like physical punches. "That's because you don't have to. You have enough on your plate."

She snorted. "Like what? I sit around all day."

"I don't think I'll be good at dating," I offered. It was true, men didn't like it when women were better with guns than they were. They had a set image for women, and leathers and guns weren't included. Besides, between killing and training, where did I have the time? "I'm happy focusing on my job."

"What about that guy you mentioned at work? Carl? You said he has the same shift as you. You guys ever pair up?"

I rolled my eyes. Carl was a bodybuilder with more interest in his own looks than the work he did. He killed to impress, not to save. And he wasn't very good at it, either. Not from where I was standing. "I prefer to work alone."

"What about Joel?"

"I'm not dating Joel. He's a great friend, but he's not really going to bring me flowers."

"That's because you wouldn't know what to do with them." She giggled. "Honestly, Adele. You're beautiful and interesting. It's a shame to waste that on work."

"What, with a scar down my neck?"

She looked down at her now-empty glass. "It's less conspicuous than a wheelchair."

It wasn't a joke this time. The cold truth hung between us, all the warmth draining out of the room. I curled my hand into a fist.

"If I hadn't gone out to the store... if I'd been able to stop him—" I started, but she shook her head.

"Don't, Adele. Don't do that to yourself." Her voice was hard but her eyes welled up. She shook her head and squeezed her eyes shut. "I'm sorry, I shouldn't have said that." She let out a shaky breath.

When she opened her eyes again any trace of crying was gone.

"Let me show you my art," she changed the topic. I got up and followed her down the passage and into her art room. She was working on an A1 canvas of a woodlands scene. Aspen was talented. She could do magic with oils and acrylic. She pointed out things on the canvas, telling me about it, but the atmosphere between us was heavy. Everything had changed with her reminder of the past. Finally I said my goodbyes, and left her house feeling worse than when I'd arrived.

My next stop was the Martial Arts Academy in Sterling Street, three blocks over. I had a meeting with the Sensei every morning at nine to train in combat and self-defense. He was the only man I'd been able to find that wouldn't treat me like a woman. He worked me to the ground, not stopping until my muscles screamed, and in hand-to-hand he put me on my back if I didn't defend myself like a man. It was the kind of training I needed. Hard, merciless.

We worked on fitness training and he had me in a good sweat. I was fit and battle ready, but he still wore me out. In hand-to-hand I went all out on him. I had pent-up frustration and anger to spare, and he was one person that would fight back but still criticize me even when I won. He put me on the floor after a failed attempt to pin him on my end, and knocked the wind out of me.

When he stood over me, he pulled up his eyebrows. He was shorter than I was standing up, but from this angle he looked larger than life. He kept his head bald and he made up for his height with muscle bulk and tone. I looked down and saw my shirt had ridden up, exposing my stomach. I had a well-toned stomach, but a bruise wrapped a decoration around my ribs. It must have happened somewhere after I'd ditched my bike.

"You been looking for trouble?" he asked. With my skillset he knew I wasn't the type to get mugged.

"Been street fighting again," I joked. "I needed a little money on the side." He grinned to cover up his concern but it was still visible when we faced off for the next round.

When we were done I collapsed on the mat, breathing hard and sweating.

"You really went all out today," I said. My ribs hurt every time I breathed in. I tried to breathe in around the pain. Ignoring it worked most of the time.

Sensei sat down next to me, cross-legged like he was going to meditate.

"You want to tell me what those bruises are about?"

I didn't really, but there were times people wouldn't let something go, and I've seen Sensei's fighting skills. If his personality matched his methods he wasn't one to let go.

I shrugged. "Occupational hazard," I finally answered. It was the truth. "I don't really have a desk job."

"I figured that," he said. "Are you in some kind of trouble?"

If he meant my life, then yes. I was in some kind of trouble every day. But it wasn't something I could just get out of the way. He wouldn't really understand.

"No, I just went about something the wrong way. It's complicated."

"Yeah, looks real complicated. Look, all I know is that you still bleed, no matter how long and hard you train to fight. Watch your back okay? I don't want to have to fill this slot with someone else because you didn't make it through."

"Nice of you to care." I didn't do care and affection. Those things were dangerous, disguises that made you feel like there were no enemies to watch your back for. Trust. That was the killer. And trust and love went hand-in-hand.

"Would be nice for you to try, too," he said and got up. Chaos averted, I told myself. It was easy to keep my cover if people didn't probe too much. There was warmth in the emptiness he left behind. Not a lot of people gave a shit, which was why I didn't, either. I rolled onto my stomach and pushed myself off, fighting the urge to try and shake of the warmth like a dog.

By noon I was back home. I found my black chain and looped in in a figure-eight over my chest and shoulders. I headed out for a run, pushing myself past the screaming muscles and aching bones. Half an hour in the dead neighborhood. I hit the shower again. I finished off with a protein shake – nothing like an after-training snack that tasted like cardboard – and crawled into bed. My body ached with the injuries and the training, but the throbbing pain reminded me I was alive, and I had to stay that way. My fingers curled around the butt of the Glock under my pillow, and only then did I relax. I never locked all my weapons away. Usually my enemies were dead by the time I walked away, but I never knew who I pissed off in the process. I kept a low profile, but luck favored the prepared.

Chapter 3

A hammering on my door pulled me out of my sleep cycle before my alarm woke me up. I stared at the hazy numbers on the digital clock next to my bed. I'd only slept about three hours. Whoever was out there had better have a bloody good reason for waking me up.

I grabbed the Glock from under my pillow and walked to the front door. I pushed my eye against the peephole. A woman with a short red bob in a power-dressing suit stood on the other side of my door. She must have been lost.

I tucked the gun into the back of my shorts' waistband, and pulled open the door.

The woman looked me up and down, and blinked. Her eyes were an emerald green and her cheeks were dusted with freckles. The black and red dress-suit made her look business-like and much too classy to be in this neighborhood.

"I'm sorry, I think I have the wrong apartment," she said, looking down at a piece of paper and then up above my door where the metal number was screwed on.

"Who are you looking for?" There weren't a lot of characters in my apartment building she wanted to see, I could tell her that much.

"Mr. Griffin?"

I cocked an eyebrow. There was no Mr. Griffin in my life.

"I'm Adele Griffin," I said. "No Mister, here. Who sent you?"

The woman looked unsure. "Ruben Cross sent me over here. He said he had an employee that could help me out."

"I work for Ruben," I said and stepped aside, making space for her to come in. If Ruben sent her to me it was business, and it was serious. She hesitated before she stepped into the apartment. I gestured toward the kitchen.

"Can I get you anything?" I asked. I opened the fridge and scanned the contents. I had to run to the store.

"Just water, thank you," she said and sat down at the booth against the wall. I shrugged and poured us each a glass. The sun was low enough to fall into my kitchen window. I wasn't usually up this time and it made me crabby.

"You're a woman," she said. Thank you Ms. Obvious.

"What do you need done?"

"I'm sorry, Ruben just didn't mention you were a woman. I expected a man."

"I can do a job as well as any man can," I said smoothly. No trace of offense – nice. If she was going to sit here and make this a sexist thing, I wasn't going to take the job, no matter who she wanted me to get rid of.

She took a sip of water. "I didn't mean that as an insult," she said. "Now that I think about it, maybe it's better that you *are* a woman. We look at things differently, don't we?"

"We certainly do," I said, sarcasm bleeding through my words. I wasn't going to be categorized. If she picked up on it she didn't react. "Who is it you want me to take care of?"

She fiddled with the glass, turning it around and around on the plastic table-top with an irritating rhythm. I placed my hand on the glass and gripped it firmly so she couldn't turn it. She looked up at me and I couldn't judge the expression on her face.

I forced politeness. "Look, this isn't a good time for me. I'm off duty, these kinds of meetings usually happen at the office. If you want me to hit someone, tell me the details so I can get back to bed."

"Hit someone?" she asked, looking confused. The ignorance of some people irritated me. You didn't knock on the door of a vampire slayer and wonder what they meant when they talked about taking care of someone.

"You're here for me to go after someone," I said, my voice snappy.

She nodded. "My fiancé."

I frowned and studied her for a second. She was very human. Her skin was light but too tan for any kind of vampire, pure-bred or half. Vampires and humans didn't mix as a rule. The few that did kept it secret, and the human-vampire couples chose to stay hidden so they wouldn't be the subject of public ridicule.

Miss Priss didn't look like the vampire type.

"I don't kill humans," I said flatly. Her eyes widened.

"Kill? I don't want you to kill anyone. I went to Ruben Cross because a colleague of mine mentioned that he deals with supernatural creatures. Connor..." Her eyes shimmered and I prayed she wouldn't cry. "Connor was kidnapped and I have reason to believe vampires did it."

I pulled up my eyebrows. Either Ruben had a twisted sense of humor, sending a rescue mission my way, or he had misunderstood this woman's idea of what his company did. I banked on the former.

"Listen, Miss..."

"Jennifer. Jennifer Lawson."

The name sounded familiar. "Jennifer. I don't do search-and-rescues. You have a problem with a vampire I can hook you up. But I don't go after their victims until they've turned."

"Is that something they'll do?"

"If the motivations are right," I said. "How long has he been missing?"

"About five days," she said. "No one has seen or heard from him, and it's unlike him to disappear without letting me know. They didn't leave a ransom note or anything, but he has a lot he can offer and a lot of people know about it."

"Vampires don't generally go after money," I said. "They recruit for power, mostly. Or secrets. You'll be surprised how much more secrets are worth."

"Secrets..." Jennifer said and I had a feeling she was talking to herself more than to me. I waited in silence for her to speak again.

"Please can you just see if you can find him? Even if he ends up being..." she swallowed hard. "Dead."

"Listen, vampires don't kill unless they have a really good reason. That's why they're allowed into society now. And if they did to him what they usually do, he'd probably have wished he was dead instead anyway. It's not legal for them to turn someone against their will, there are laws about these things although I can't say they're set in stone yet. There are a lot of loopholes when it comes down to vampires. I'm very sorry for your loss, but these things happen, and unfortunately there's not a lot I can do about it. Not until he pops up on my radar as a vampire, and I have an order to take him out."

Tears spilled over her cheeks and I groaned inwardly. She clipped open a black handbag and rummaged around in it until she pulled out a tissue. She ran it underneath her eyes so her make-up wouldn't smudge.

"I'll pay you whatever you like," she said. "I just need to get him back. Or at least know what happened to him if I don't."

"And if it turns out he's a vampire? Because it's more than likely that that is what happened to him."

She shuddered. There were cases where humans married vampires and families with them. I was living proof of that. But there was a new category of racism among humans and vampires too, where they discriminated because of newfound differences. It didn't look to me like Jennifer was the type that would get it on with a vampire – it took a bit more of an open mind than she seemed to have for that one – but people often surprised me.

"I don't suppose there are ways to save them?" she asked.

"Save?" If she thought that being a vampire was some sort of curse that needed saving from, she had another thing coming. But it wasn't my style to defend vampires, considering that I hunted them, so I kept my mouth shut and pushed the underlying offense aside.

"Unfortunately there's not a lot we can do about it," I said instead. "Once he's a vampire, there's not really going back."

"It's his soul, isn't it?" she said in a whisper. "It's lost now."

I fought the urge to roll my eyes. The idea that vampires were the undead who had no soul was a common misconception. I blamed literature. There were so many stories claiming things about vampires that weren't really true. People tended to categorize them based on a few corresponding facts, like sunlight and fangs, and they missed the rest of the information.

"Vampires aren't undead, Jennifer," I said, trying to explain. "They're living, just like you and me."

"Then what happens when they're turned?" she asked.

"It's more like a mutation. A virus that alters them. Permanently. They need different things to survive like darkness and blood, and their bodies change because of new lifestyles and diets. Think more along the lines of a different set of hormones kicking in. Blood loss is what turns them."

The fact that it messed with their moral structures too was something no one had been able to explain yet. In my books that was what set them apart from humans. Something happened to them, the humanity got taken away, and an unfeeling monster stayed behind, willing to kill, willing to sacrifice despite love.

Maybe that was the bit where humans had attributed the quality of the 'undead' to them. The bit where they were heartless had translated into literally 'not having a heart'. But the facts were that vampires were alive, unless I got my hands on them.

Jennifer starting sniveling again and I felt the onset of a black mood. Give me lack of sleep and a crying woman and I'm ready for my next kill.

"Will you help me?" she asked. "You're the last person I can turn to. No one else in my world really believes in the underworld – the whole thing is a bit bizarre to most people."

I kept quiet. In my experience, the longer I didn't say anything, the more the other person filled up the empty space with their own words.

"Do you follow news, Miss Griffin?" she asked.

I shook my head. She nodded hers.

"There's just been a bit of trouble with his company lately. A lot of ugly things came out that were painted the wrong way. I think it's all an inside job to pin it on Connor."

"Why would anyone want to do that?"

"He stands for vampires and their rights. A lot of people are angry about it."

"But you're saying vampires did it. That doesn't make sense."

She shrugged and it looked like she was searching for words. She kept her eyes on her hands, fiddling with the tissue she'd used for her tears.

"He just employed the wrong people," she finally said. "He didn't do anything to deserve this. Oh god, what if they do end up just killing him?"

I crossed my arms over my chest and leaned back in my seat, feeling the Glock bite into my back. I didn't do pity cases, but this guy was a human. Well, he had been before he'd been taken. If he still was, it was my duty at least to try and protect him. If he wasn't, it wasn't my problem until Ruben made it mine. But I had other things on my plate. I had to deal with so much already, and someone's kidnapping wasn't really in my job description.

"Do you mind if I ask what your motivation is?" I said. I didn't like taking on jobs that didn't fit into my division.

"Didn't I just explain my motivation?" she asked. She looked confused like I'd said something foreign. "How much of a reason do you need to get your loved one back? Connor and I are engaged. He's so much a part of my life I can't imagine my life without it. Haven't you ever loved so much that it felt like you were bleeding to death when something happened to them? Like half of you doesn't work right anymore?"

I thought of Aspen. Maybe. But she didn't talk about that kind of love.

"I'm not just going to go on a wild-goose-chase if I don't know what I'm doing this for. Is he in trouble himself or is it his company?"

She opened her mouth and moved it without words coming out before she finally closed it again and just shook her head.

"It's all on the company," she said. "He didn't do anything wrong."

Jennifer studied her perfectly manicured nails intently. I wondered where people got time in the world for things like that. Between surviving and training to survive I didn't have a lot of time to bother with my looks.

She opened her mouth but hesitated before she finally spoke.

"I love him," she said quietly. "Shouldn't that be enough?"

I supposed it was. I loved Aspen and she was the drive for all of this. But I didn't understand how men and women loved each other enough for something like that. All I knew about love was the fact that it could kill you. Literally.

Jennifer looked at me with impossibly green eyes. Had Ruben sent her to me because he knew the moral side of it would get to me? Was it about the money? Or did he really think she had a job for me? She was pretty straightforward about what she wanted. I doubted Ruben misunderstood. He was obtuse but he wasn't stupid.

"Look, let me think about this. I'll give you an answer by tomorrow." I wanted to turn it down. I wanted to stay away from this mess. Love stories didn't do it for me, and I didn't want to have to deal with sniveling women who'd lost their boyfriends. It was tough all over, if I sat here dribbling about everything I'd lost I wouldn't ever get out of the house.

But something in me drew to it like a magnet. The pull fascinated me as much as it bugged me.

Jennifer nodded. She looked disappointed, but she didn't say it. The truth was that I just didn't know. My loyalty lay with humans, but I didn't generally get involved with people unless it involved killing. And I didn't get involved with vampires unless there was a 'wanted' sign on their backs. If I could choose they'd all have that, but again it wasn't my thing to kill those that didn't do something to deserve it.

Jennifer opened her handbag again and pulled out a business card, sliding it across the table.

"This is where you can reach me," she said. I turned the card and looked it over. She was a marketing consultant at the big shot firm with the glass exterior in the heart of the CBD. The Palace, they called it. I'd seen it before. Chances were her boyfriend was a big shot too.

"What did you say his name was?"

"Connor O'Neill," she said.

Definitely a big shot. I'd heard of him, his name was in the news every now and then, but for what I didn't know. I only listened to the news to hear if there were any bulletins on vampire killing that would cue me to lay low.

Jennifer stood up. I let her walk to the door first. I made a point of not having someone at my back, ever. Even if they were small and harmless, like Jennifer. It was a good rule to live by, and it made me uncomfortable to break it. Sometimes it was the small, harmless looking ones that did the most damage. Besides, I didn't want to give her a look at the gun I had on me. She wouldn't have been able to miss the black matte metal against my white tank.

"Thank you," she said as she stepped through the door.

"I'll call you," I promised when she was outside and half-turned to me. "Are you going to be alright getting out of here? It's not the best neighborhood."

"I have a car waiting in the street," she said, and turned away. A car. Waiting. Imagine that.

I closed the door and walked back to the room. I returned my Glock to its place under my pillow, and pulled the sheets over me.

I closed my eyes, but my mind was awake now, and whirring. The vampire in the alley came back to me, it's accusing eyes. I felt like a low-life, betraying them. But then again, which species had been the traitor when I'd lost my mother and nearly Aspen, too? My circumstances had created me, and a killing vampire had made me a vampire killer. I wasn't going to apologize for taking care of Aspen.

I buried my face in the pillow and forced my mind to be a blank until I finally fell asleep again.

Chapter 4

The office lights at Cross Ledger Accounting were on but the lobby lights were off, making it look like offices were closed but a handful of people were putting in some overtime. I walked through to the office Sonya used when the sun set. Sonya was a vampire. With her mouse-brown hair and dull yellow eyes her pale skin made her look even more washed out. She was impossibly thin and tall, with long fingers. Ruben employed her because it meant he could take vampire business then, too, if it came down to it. I didn't understand how he thought. Money was the drive behind his choices. I guessed that involved both sides, then. Vampires often had a lot more money because they stuck around for long enough to make fortunes. Immortality was both a blessing and a curse.

I put my helmet on Sony's desk. She glanced up at me, irritated. Her lips lifted in a snarl that threatened to roll back over her long fangs, but she controlled herself. You just didn't show your fangs to a vampire killer. She knew well enough what I could do.

"Ruben wants to see you before you head out," she said, handing me a stack of papers. I flipped through them. We were careful not to touch each other in the exchange. Her skin on mine felt like it would burn me. I was sure she felt the same about me. The papers had photos of driver's licenses or black and white scans pulled off servers somewhere.

"Who's this one?" I asked. There was no photo, only a social security number.

"That's the one Ruben wants to see you about," Sonya said, not looking up at me. "He's in his office."

Where else would he be? I took the stack of papers and walked into Ruben's office. He was scribbling something down on a piece of paper.

"Since when do you send clients to my apartment?" I asked. I didn't sit down, and in my leathers and lace ups I was intimidating. Ruben knew I carried fire power, and I didn't know if he was sure I wouldn't use it.

"Look, she wouldn't leave me alone. She kept on about needing to find some vampire and you're the best person for that kind of thing. Besides, she was going to pay big bucks. I wasn't going to pass her up."

"No, you were going to pass her *on*. She wants a rescue mission. I don't do charity cases."

Ruben looked up at me. "She said she'd pay."

"I didn't mean money. I meant letting people live. It's not my department."

Ruben chuckled and dropped his pen. "Look, you do what you want with that case, but make it look like you did what you could so I can get some money out of this. Miss Lawson is willing to pay big bucks for this, I don't hire you for my health."

I grunted and sat down on a chair opposite him.

"What about this other one? Sonya was cheerful about it." Sonya was never cheerful about anything. Maybe working as a vampire in a firm that slayed them after hours was a touchy subject. I doubted she did it for the money. Ruben paid her next to nothing. How could she not care that her own kind was being killed off? Maybe she had a reason to hate them the same way I did.

"Someone from the Hills wants this one taken out. Another big contract, he's a big shot around town that did something to piss off the wrong people. I want you all out on this one. It's a kill so it will be right up your alley."

"What am I supposed to do with this?" I lifted up the paper with the details. "You didn't give me much to work with. I don't even have a name or an address."

Ruben shrugged. "That's what they gave me, they're not too keen on any of this information getting out. They're trying to limit the amount of information that passes hands around here, I get the feeling they're after him for something bigger than the usual I-hate-vampires stuff. You've done this before. Don't tell me you're getting picky. Picky is above your pay-grade."

I rolled my eyes and got up. My fingers itched to get my hands on a vampire or two. I was in a terrible mood and the only way to fix that was to take out a menace.

"Don't cut it so close, I want to leave the office earlier tonight."

"If I believe you had what it took to set foot in the dark, I'd believe you," I called over my shoulder. Ruben could suck it. I did what I wanted. He wasn't going to fire me, Carl was a joke and Ruben would lose all his money. There weren't a lot of people out there jumping for this job opportunity.

Sonya shook her head when I walked past. I took my helmet off her desk and stepped out into the night.

The air was crisp with the first hints of autumn hanging in the air. There were no clouds, and the sky was filled with pin-pricks of light. I opened throttle and drove to the first address on my list. A driver's license was a lot of help – I found houses that way – but the vampires were hardly home.

I stopped in front of a red brick house with a well maintained lawn. The night smelled like Jasmine when I walked across to the front door. Vampires liked to choose night scented flowers, not because they liked them but because any animal knew the importance of scents and covering them up. The porch light was on but everything else was off, and emptiness hung in the air.

I walked around the back of the house. I kept my eyes open for trouble, but my nose worked overtime. There was no vampire on the premises. The smell of cheap cologne hung in the air near the bedroom window, telling me the vampire had been here earlier and tried to douse his scent with a different smell. They tended to do that. Vampires could smell each other out, and cologne helped. But it wasn't enough.

It was never enough.

I worked my blade under one of the windows at the back and slid it up. It was a good neighborhood and the windows weren't sticky like some of the ones I worked with. It also helped that there were no burglar bars. Those could really make breaking-and-entering a bitch.

Inside the house I walked around. The furniture was cheap but nice, and organized like the person liked being here. I guessed that this had been the house it had stayed in before it'd turned. Vampires often chose a new place because they cut ties with their old life, and often the interiors changed. They were asleep when they were home in daytime, and at night they wanted to get out. The night air made vampire skins itch if they were cooped up for too long.

Houses became a safe shelter from the sun for sleep. Furniture and décor didn't matter.

The en-suite bathroom was the room with the fragrance hanging thick in the air. It tickled my nose and I crinkled it, trying to breathe around the smell. In the bedroom I found what I was looking for. A scent that wasn't altered. The bed was full of it. The myth that vampires slept in coffins was absolutely ridiculous. Vampires liked comfort as much as the next person. The curtains in front of the window were thick and black, with roll-up blinds. I looked carefully at the walls around the window.

Shutters had been installed that came down in daytime to keep out the light, but it was well done. Classy.

"Well, let's see if we can find you," I said and took a deep breath, filling my nose with the scent. It smelled like earth and mulch, and something that reminded me of baby-powder even though I couldn't compare the smells. I didn't know what did it. Maybe the powdery quality of something that could live longer than your average eighty years.

The house had little else to offer. There were no photos or personal mementos that I could see. This vampire had fallen into the habit of distancing itself from life a little after all.

Finding the vampire after I left the house was easy. It was a matter of tracking. The scent was easy to pick up. The vampire had left over the back wall and not through the front yard. Clever.

I found its scent on the other side of the wall and followed it through two neighboring gardens. I stuck to the shadows and kept my ears open, but I wouldn't be seen. Unless there were dogs it was easy to hide myself.

Animals were a whole different ball game. Some animals loved vampires. They were drawn to the lack of human presence in the vampires' nature. Other animals hated them. With me it could swing both ways. Animals hated or loved me depending on how much of me showed to them, and which side they preferred. I hated that it was a gamble and I could never be sure, but I had enough going for me that I couldn't complain about a few setbacks. After all, everyone had flaws.

The vampire was a young one. It didn't cover itself up the way it should have, and I found it two blocks away. It was hunched in a corner, eyes half-closed with the satiated high of the feed. If you've ever seen a snake with an animal half-down its throat you'd get the idea. There was a moment for every predator where it was helpless. For a vampire it was the moment just after a feed, when the energy levels hadn't kicked up just yet, and the vampire was lulled into a passive state for a just a few counts.

It was my luck that I'd caught it at the perfect moment. I waited until it snapped back to reality so that it would have a fighting chance, but even then the vampire wasn't as quick as it should have been. It was clumsy and helpless and it didn't take long before the job was done. I didn't even get my leathers dirty.

I walked away, unsatisfied and more frustrated than when I'd started.

I had a handful of vampires still to find for the night, but I needed a challenge. If it wasn't a good fight, if I didn't have to fight for my life, it wasn't worth it. There was nothing that made me feel as alive as being so close to death I could smell the rot on its breath.

I was going to find the faceless vampire that Ruben wanted me to hunt down. That would be a challenge, and I had all night to do it.

When I got to my bike my phone rang.

"Are you knee-deep in blood yet, or can you come in?" It was Joel. "Your ammunition arrived and I have another gun here that's looking for an owner that will actually fire it."

"It's a slow night. I've got time. I need you for a couple of things, anyway. I'll be there in ten."

I pulled my helmet on my head and turned the throttle, spraying gravel like waves on both sides until I was on the street. I got to Joel in less than ten minutes. When I pulled into the drive the garage door was already open for me. I rolled my bike inside and the automatic doors slowly rolled shut.

"You're going to get caught if you draw attention to yourself like that," Joel said.

"What, and you don't think I can talk my way out of it?" I pouted and made my eyes big. He laughed and hugged me. His dark brown hair was long and curled where it brushed his shoulders and jawline. He wore glasses with a black frame that made his eyes stand out, and he always had a three-day stubble. Today he wore sweatpants and a matching jacket with holes cut in the sleeves for his thumbs, but I'd seen him in a variety of outfits ranging from hobo to classy. Joel was weird, but there were no questions about who he was, and his loyalty was complete. He would never rat me out.

"Come on through," he said. We walked through a narrow door at the back of the garage. It led into a small room with a narrow strip of small windows against the ceiling. Servants' quarters once upon a time. A dark opening took up most of the floor space with a concrete staircase leading down into the earth. The trap door leaned up against the wall. There were houses in Westham that still had war bunkers and the like. Joel had been lucky enough to snatch one of the last ones on the market.

Fluorescent lights hung from the ceiling every couple of feet, throwing circles of light on several work benches. The low hum of the lights filled the air and classical music streamed from a radio somewhere.

He opened a safe, and stacked boxes of ammo onto the table in front of me. The boxes all had polystyrene packaging in them with rows of bullets. Five by ten. Joel packed them out according to their labels.

"Smith and Wesson 500s, Gen4 Glock 23, 9mm Beretta, SIG Sauer P226."

I nodded as he named them. He knew what I carried. Joel Garber was the only person in the county that could organize silver bullets. If you asked me every police officer needed to carry at least one cartridge of silver, not only the vampire-prison guards, but vampires hadn't made that kind of name for themselves yet.

"You're a star," I said, taking out cartridges I had on me and filling them. The rest I would put in the storage compartment on my bike. I always felt better when I had a fresh set of ammo.

"Should last you a while," Joel said.

"I hope so."

Joel walked to the narrow locker in the corner and opened it. He took out a gun and walked back to me.

I whistled, taking it from him. It was a Carbine AR-15. The black metal was cold under my fingers.

"This one's semi-automatic. Air-cooled. Light enough for you to throw around when you need to." He produced a scope. "And it has extras."

I smiled, looking the gun over, holding it up against my shoulder to try it on for size. It was light, Joel was right.

"Not your usual inconspicuous deal, but I thought you could appreciate it."

"This is why I love coming to you," I said, grinning. Joel pushed a box of ammo across the table toward me. "And you got me silver for it," I exclaimed. Joel grinned.

"What else do you need done?" He leaned back against the desk and folded his arms.

"I need you to check out a social security number for me. It's all I have to go by."

Joel shook his head but he walked to his computer and sat down. It was always on. He ran a hell of a system. I didn't know much about these things but Joel was a real techy. Sometimes I wondered what he did in a hole in Westham, helping a fly-by-night vampire hunter like me.

"Don't you have better things to do with your time?" I asked. He held out his hand and I gave him the paper with the details on it. He kept his eyes on the screen while his fingers flew over the keyboard in a blur.

"Then who are you going to run to for this information? There are some ugly characters in town."

I snorted. "I think I count as one of them," I said. He grinned.

"You're not so bad. I've seen worse. You don't see the kinds of guys that walk through my door."

"If they don't have fangs they're not really on my radar," I agreed. Joel and I were tight and we'd come a long way.

"Here we are," Joel said and the computer beeped. I walked around the desk and bent down. My face hovered over Joel's shoulder. He smelled musky, like he'd sprayed on deodorant, but not recently.

"There's no name," I said. It was only an address. 442 Caldwell Street. It was definitely in Westham Hills.

"I know. His details are blocked with all sorts of firewalls and security systems. This was all I could get."

"I thought you were good at this," I teased.

He turned and looked at me. His face was open and his eyes serious. He was offended.

"I can do it, but it's going to take me a while. You don't look like you want to wait a day or two."

I shook my head. "I'll figure it out."

Joel nodded and got up. "Look, I'll keep running it for you and let you know if I find anything else. Until then you're going to have to use address only. It's more than you started off with, though."

I climbed the stairs back up to the garage, carrying my load. Joel followed. I packed my ammunition into the compartment under the seat, and swung my leg over. The Carbine was on my back with a strap. There was nowhere else I could put it with the compartment full, but maybe I could get the chance to use it tonight. I was about to pull my helmet onto my head when Joel put his hand on my arm.

"Be careful out there," he said.

"I have at least two hundred shots on me and a helluva gun. Don't worry about it."

"People don't usually have that kind of protection unless it's serious. He doesn't want to be found, and you're going to push his buttons by doing the exact opposite. Don't get dead."

"I won't," I said, smiling at Joel. I wasn't going to tell him that if that happened, I didn't know if I'd be too upset about it. They couldn't turn me with my already-vampire mix of blood. The only way for me to go was out for good. Sometimes I wondered if it would really be a bad thing. Still, his concern was endearing. I pulled my helmet onto my head and waited for the garage door to roll up. I pulled into the night, my bike the only sound for miles around.

I opened throttle and raced down the street. I followed the main road until I had to take a left that eventually wound up the hill. It became darker, the halos around the lights drowned in the canopy of leaves that stretched over the road and around the lights. My bike's headlight cut a shaft of light into the inky black, and the darkness folded closed behind me again like a curtain.

I found Caldwell Street easily. It was close to the top of the hill. The road was framed by high walls with electric fencing on top and cast iron gates with intricate curls to keep everyone out that didn't belong. Through the gates I spied mansions, lit up by green garden lighting and chandelier porch lights, making the rest of Westham look like someone's leftovers.

Number 442 had a mustard-colored nine foot wall all around it, and it was topped off with electric fencing. The gate was big and black, mostly solid so I couldn't see much through it save for the kind of paving on the other side. The spikes on top were a warning. With all my skills and breaking-and-entering expertise I wasn't sure how I was going to get into this one. I sat back on the seat of my motorbike in the dark shadows of a huge poplar tree, and listened.

The whole neighborhood was alive, I could feel people everywhere. They felt like warm puffs of air that clouded around your face in winter. Smells travelled to me on the wind, sweet and spicy, a mix of people and the lifeblood pumping through their veins. There was no way I was going to find a trace of this vampire by sitting in the road. Either I had to make another plan, or I had to wait a day or two for Joel to get back to me.

I hated waiting. I had a furnace raging inside of me that only managed to settle after a kill. I couldn't get the burning heat under my skin to stop without it.

I leaned forward and I was about to turn the key to kick the engine into life when a dark shadow blurred in the corner of my eye. I was too late, the sight reaching my brain too slowly. Something hard knocked me on the right of my jaw and I crashed to the ground next to my bike. White spots danced in front of my eyes and for a moment I couldn't figure out which way was up. The world spun around me and I was nauseous, like I was going to heave out my stomach.

I pushed myself up on my hands and knees. I had to be fight-ready - I was sure there would be a follow-up - but with my head spinning I wasn't worth much. With my one had I reached for the Carbine on my back and pointed it deftly in front of me while I pushed myself up. Joel would be happy to hear it was fired first night on the job.

I heard a snicker to my left, and I swung the gun in that direction, but I couldn't see anything.

My mind recovered and I was up on my feet with a swift jump. The air smelled stale, laced with a flowery scent I couldn't place - it tried to be natural, but it wasn't. I pulled the trigger and the first bullets left the barrel with a whoosh and a clap, but whatever was out there moved. I could feel it in the atmosphere, a shift. If this person was faster than my bullets I was in trouble. If I was too concussed to shoot straight, I was in trouble too, but I could forgive myself for that.

"You're not nearly what I thought you'd be," a silky voice traveled to me on the breeze. It surrounded me and caressed my skin, a whisper that physically touched me. A woman's voice. An icy finger traced a shiver down my spine.

She stepped into a pool of moonlight that broke through the leaves. She was dressed in tight black clothes - it looked like I wasn't the only one that dressed to suit the night - and she had white hair that was pulled back tightly against her head. She kept her head dipped so her face was masked with shadows. Where her eyes should have been there were only pools of black.

"Who are you?" I asked. I didn't usually ask my opponents that, but then again, they'd never been the ones to hunt *me*.

"Your worst nightmare," she said, and the cliché was lost in the venom in her voice.

We circled each other in a crouched stance, both ready to attack. I still had the gun pointed in her direction. One pull of the trigger and she would have a hole in her chest, human or not. I had my mind back in the game so she wouldn't be able to outrun them again. But I was intrigued by this woman, this person who managed to seem like a copy of me, and the exact opposite, all at once.

"What do you want?" I asked. The million dollar question.

"How long did you think you could get away with it? How long did you think it was going to take for people to find out what you really are?"

Blood drained from my face and I suddenly felt cold, despite my leather jacket. I'd hoped the answer to those would be 'never'. There was a reason I worked in the dead hours of the night.

I opened my mouth to ask a question but she launched at me. She took me by surprise again. Twice in one night - I was getting sloppy. In the process she knocked my gun out of my hand and it clattered into the darkness beyond my reach. There was no time for me to reach for another gun. She was on top of me, and she didn't fight like a girl.

I silently thanked Sensei for training me the way he did. It got dirty fast. Her fists were like jackhammers, with a strength that equaled my own. I wondered if she was human, or some other sort of creature. A half-breed like me, or maybe something else that was mythical. Vampires might have been the only creatures acknowledged by the government, but there were others, too. They just kept it very quiet because it was still a myth everywhere.

We rolled around in the dirt. She got more hits in than I did, and besides it hurting, it made me angry. I never even got beaten up by man. How was a girl beating me?

I was on the floor, and she was taking out whatever she had against me on my face. I saw stars. I reached down and pulled out my knife from the thigh sheath. I lunged at her but she was faster than I thought and I only nicked her skin. Still, she let out a piercing scream and let me go, scrambling away.

"Bitch," she said to me in what sounded a lot like a hiss. "You better watch your back, this isn't over." She melted into the shadows, and two seconds later she was gone. Silver had saved me many times before, and if she'd reacted to it that badly, she was definitely not human. Or a half-bred vampire. I was fine with silver.

I groaned and laid back on the tarmac. My face throbbed and ached. I touched my nose carefully and my fingers came away with blood, black in the moonlight.

I rolled over and pushed myself up, every muscle screaming in protest. I managed to get myself back into Westham downtown where the streetlights were welcome and the roads were familiar. I knew nothing could get to me out here.

"What the hell happened to you?" Ruben asked when I walked into the office. He checked his watch. "You're early."

"Yeah I think I'm going to call it a night," I said. I dropped the ID of the one vampire I'd gotten on his desk. He raised his eyebrows.

"Before you say it," I said when I saw a complaint forming on his tongue. "You want to send me out there to do your dirty work you better bank on it that I'm going to take some time off to recover. Any other job has sick leave."

"And other jobs pay tax," he said.

"I'm going home. I'll call you," I answered and walked out. Sonya didn't say anything. She just stared. I bet she was damn happy about her safe little desk job.

I made my way home slower than usual. I didn't want to run into a pole because my coordination was off. I was dizzy and I felt nauseous, the movement around me made it worse. I was sure I would have a concussion. I considered myself lucky I didn't have a broken nose. Small blessings.

I made it home and into the shower. The water stung on my face. I had a split lip and I would have a black eye and a swollen jaw for a day or two. Nothing as pretty as girl after a cat fight. Thank goodness for healing abilities. When I looked in the mirror my colorful face complimented the scar down my neck for a change, and it blended rather than stood out. I shook my head at myself but I stopped again. My brain felt like it was loose in my head.

I fell into bed. I had the mind to check my Glock before I put my head onto the pillow, and I let myself sink into a deep slumber.

Chapter 5

When I woke up again the light in my bedroom was all wrong. It was way past sunrise. I checked the clock on my nightstand and swore. I'd missed my class with Sensei and I had a missed call from Aspen on my phone. I pushed myself up and swore again when all my muscles screamed in protest. Sore muscles weren't a new thing for me with how hard I trained, but there was a hell of a difference between lactic acid and bruises.

I picked up the phone and dialed Aspen's number.

"Are you okay?" she asked when she picked up. "When you weren't here I was worried."

"I had a rough night and slept it off. I'm sorry I didn't let you know. I'll be over later."

I phoned Sensei as well and rescheduled. I was relieved I hadn't ended up going. I was stupid enough to train even when I was injured, and it wouldn't have worked out well for me. The only reason I didn't go now was because he didn't have any other free slots on a Wednesday.

When I looked at my reflection in the mirror in the light of day I looked better than expected. My eye was still bruised but it looked like the worst was over. Instead of an angry purple the way humans would have, it was a yellowy-blue like when it was healing. My split lip was healed, just tender. My head still hurt like hell. I tried to imagine what I would look like if I were a human.

An image of Aspen on the floor in a pool of blood flashed in front of my eyes. A cut across her forehead, the blood slick and glistening on her cheek and the carpet. Teeth, sharp and elongated, and the guttural hiss that meant it was going to strike again. The slump form of my mother's body under the table, the lifeless eyes staring through me.

Well, that wasn't what I'd wanted to see. I squeezed my eyes shut and grunted, grinding my teeth hard enough for my jaw to hurt. Pain grounded me when violence couldn't. I had to get out of the house, get away from the memories.

When I finally made it to the other side of Westham it was almost eleven and my internal clock was shot. I knocked on the door and Zelda opened. When she saw me she pulled up her eyebrows.

"What happened to you?" she asked. I shrugged. "One of them got to me." What was I going to say? I was getting into trouble and it was literally starting to bite me in the ass. Aspen was in her art room when I found her. She looked up at me, her face bright and open, but when she saw me the light dimmed in her eyes. She frowned.

"Did you have a rough night?" Well, you could have said that. I didn't look so bad but she knew I was healing fast enough for it to have been bad.

I shook my head and forced a smile. "It looks a lot worse than it feels," I lied. It felt like hell. It was more emotional than physical at this point though. "In my line of work these things happen once in a while."

Aspen pursed her lips into a thin line and her eyes became impossibly big, shimmering.

"Don't worry about me. I just had to come see you so you would know I'm alright." I wasn't sure if this would count as alright in her books. The truth was I'd come to see her to make sure she was the one that was alright.

"Have you had anyone contact you lately?" I asked.

"Contact me? How?" When she frowned and tipped her head to the side like that she looked exactly like she did when she was fourteen. Sometimes Aspen didn't age a day. It was what made her so vulnerable. Even before she'd been wheelchair bound.

"Don't worry about it," I said, shrugging to look less serious. "Someone mentioned something yesterday about half-breeds."

"You mean that we're going to be thrown out in the open?" she asked.

"I doubt that's going to happen. Just tell me if anyone tries to call or anything, okay?"

It wasn't her they were after. It was me. Aspen wasn't a threat because she didn't go out there looking for trouble. I was the one the woman from last night was after. It was because I was leaving a trail, however thin, and it was something someone could follow.

I swallowed hard and pushed the guilt away that throbbed in my gut. If I was caught or discovered somehow it would put Aspen in danger. And that would be the exact opposite of what I was trying to do every night.

The only answer was to be careful and to keep an eye out for my attacker. And if it happened again, I wouldn't lose. Not again. Only one person would walk away next time.

"I wanted to talk to you about something," I said, changing the subject. "I need your help."

"Oh, the great Adele comes to me for help?" Aspen said, beaming.

"Don't get a big head," I said, but the light was back in her eyes and she radiated warmth. This was how I liked her. This was how she was meant to be.

I told her about Jennifer and her job for me.

"Isn't this the kind of thing you're supposed to be doing?" Aspen asked. Oh right, the police job I used as a front. In that case it would have made sense.

"It's not exactly in my line of work," I answered. Not at all, actually. "I was wondering if I should take it anyway."

"I think you should," she said.

"Why?"

"Because of how you told me that it's probably the right thing to do. You seem convinced that it is, and that's as good a reason as any. Besides, if vampires got this guy... it might be too late for him. He might be..."

"I know," I said softly. We were both influenced by what had happened to us. We couldn't think of vampires the same anymore, no matter how related we ended up being. Aspen painted her emotions. I fought them out. To each their own, but we both had the same problem.

"You have to save him, if you can," Aspen said, and her voice was different. Thick like she was going to cry.

"And if I can't?"

She shrugged. There wasn't an answer she could give me, but I didn't need one for that question from her. I could answer it for myself – kill him.

"Thank you," I said and got up, planting a kiss on her hair. "I'll see you tomorrow."

"Let me know if something comes up again. I worry about you."

"I will," I said and let myself out. It was sweet of her to worry about me. She didn't have to. I worried enough for the both of us.

On the bus back home I took out my phone and fished the business card out of my wallet. I dialed the number and waited. After the third ring an older voice picked up.

"Jennifer Lawson's office."

"I'd like to speak to Jennifer please," I said. "Tell her it's Adele Griffin calling."

Music blared over the line for a moment, and then Jennifer's crisp voice rang out over the speaker.

"I was beginning to think you'd given up on me," she said. "I'm so glad you called."

"I'll do it," I said to her. She gasped into the phone and then her voice changed so it made me think she was getting emotional on me again.

"Look, you have to give me something to work with," I said before she could get blubbery on me. "A photo would be great, but more information like places he liked to go, an address maybe. You know, the important things. Anything that will help me find this guy as quickly as I can."

"Of course, I'll send it to you. Do you have an e-mail address?"

I gave her my home e-mail. I hardly every used it, I preferred to deal with my clients face-to-face in most cases. I would check later.

I hung up the phone. Just as I did it rang in my hands, and I pushed the talk button.

"Joel," I said.

"I have a hit on that social security number you were asking about. Do you want to swing by tonight to have a look?" Great. A kill was exactly what I needed.

"You're a saint, Joel. I'll be there just after sunset."

I ended the conversation and hung up. It looked like it was going to be a good night. I dialed one more number. Sonya answered the phone, and when she heard it was me her words became clipped.

"He's in a meeting," she said.

"Just tell him I'm coming in tonight, but I'll be a bit late." I wasn't going to beg to talk to Ruben. He wasn't my favorite, and if it weren't for my job I would choose never to see him again.

At home I made a sandwich for lunch and switched on the computer I hardly ever used. A thick sheet of dust lay over the top, and it took a long time to think about it before it booted. One e-mail waited for me in my inbox. It had Jennifer Lawson's letterhead boldly at the top and it was flagged urgent and private. I wondered if she knew that this address was so unused I doubted anyone would know about it to hack the information.

I opened the e-mail. His name was Connor O'Neill, as she'd told me. A photo was attached of a young man with blond hair and a lot of muscle, but not in a showy way. It was lean muscle.

Strength. His eyes were blue like the ocean, smiling at me. If I ever paid attention to that kind of quality in a man I had to admit he was attractive. He had the same glossiness about him that Jennifer had, the sheen that accompanied the rich. There was something very familiar about him, but I couldn't place where I'd seen him before. His eyes were captivating, even in the photo.

The address listed was 13 Mulberry drive. It was in an average neighborhood just this side of the business district. Nothing too rich and fancy, nothing that screamed social elite. She'd added a couple of his favorite hangouts and business meeting places, all very public and posh.

That troubled me. If the address didn't make sense, it might have been new. New addresses pointed to vampire changes, especially if they tried so hard to be inconspicuous. To me, nothing stood out more than a vampire trying to blend in.

I sent the information to Joel to print out for when I got there. If anything had happened to Connor O'Neill all that information would be pretty useless, but it was a place to start at least. I wished I had a shirt or something with his smell. I wasn't going to ask Jennifer for it. One way to betray your true identity was to act like a bloodhound and look like a human. Maybe the house in Mulberry Street would have something to offer. Jennifer was going to have to stay in the dark about my identity no matter how far that set me back in my search.

Chapter 6

By sunset I was ready to roll. I pulled my black leather jacket over the shoulder holster. I had the Smith & Wesson on me, freshly loaded with gleaming silver bullets. I wasn't going to take chances with a smaller gun. At my back I had my SIG and my knife was in its thigh sheath I didn't want another run-in with GI Jane, if she came at me again, I would get her.

Still I felt naked. I wondered if it would be suspicious if I drove around with the Carbine on my back again, but I decided against it. The S&W would pack the right kind of punch if it came down to it, and Carbine hadn't helped the night before.

I'd applied make-up around my eye and on my jaw to cover up the yellowish smudge the bruises had gone down to, but it looked wrong. The color was wrong for my skin tone. I washed it off again. I didn't care about what I looked like but I didn't want to run around looking like I was obviously trying to cover something up.

My phone vibrated in my pocket as I walked out the door.

"The reporter was here again today," Ruben's gravelly voice scraped through the speaker.

"You sure she doesn't just want to write a review on your excellent accounting skills?" Ruben's firm had a good name and he was charming enough to fool people who didn't know enough. Reporters fell in the 'ignorant' bracket – for all their research they ended up empty-handed almost every time.

"This one's not letting go. She keeps insisting to pop by after hours, doesn't want to take it when I tell her the offices are closed."

"Well, you are in the business of doing accounts for some vampires. Maybe it's about that. But I'll watch out," I said. I slid one leg over my bike and straddled it. "I'll come in in about an hour."

I hung up before he could argue with me. This was business, after all. He'd pointed Jennifer in my direction, he would pay me for my time to play good cop.

I slipped my phone into my jacket pocket and pulled the helmet over my hair.

Joel was waiting for me in his open garage when I arrived, and I pulled in.

"What happened to you?" he asked the moment I took my helmet off. He knew too that I healed up fast. He was doing the math. I wondered if I should have covered up after all.

"Someone's on my trail," I admitted. I could say something like that to Joel. He looked concerned and lifted his hand to my face. His fingers brushed the skin under my eye, and small jolts of electricity travelled into my skin when he did. Maybe in a different life something more could have happened between us.

"It's nothing. Just looks bad," I said, leaning back so he wouldn't touch me anymore. I wasn't good with physical touch.

"You need to up your training skills if you're going to be fighting your victims like this."

"It wasn't a victim. She said something about getting away with who I am, but to be honest I was getting beaten up too much to follow conversation."

"She?"

I nodded. "Turns out I'm not the only girl that can fight like a man. If a woman punches without concern for a broken nail you must know you passed the cat-fight chapter."

Joel shook his head and turned toward the door, expecting me to follow. I did.

"You're going to run yourself into a corner one of these days," he said over his shoulder.

I shrugged but he couldn't see it, and stepped into the stairwell.

The place looked neater than the night before, and I wondered vaguely if he had domestic help that he let down here once in a while. I didn't trust anyone with my equipment, but maybe he had found someone he could rely on. To each his own. Trust in general wasn't my strong suit.

Joel sat down in front of his computer. The bluish light fell on his face and colored his skin to a greenish color, making him seem bruised, like me. Or alien.

"I didn't get much for you, the system is still a tough one to crack. Whatever they're using, it's top of the range and the newest around. My software could only do so much."

"I didn't know you could be outsmarted," I teased. Joel prided himself by his ability to get into any system in the world if he had to.

"Are you trying to be funny?" he asked. "Because you're not."

His fingers clacked on the keys and windows popped open on the screen.

"Did you get the e-mail I forwarded to you?" I asked.

"I printed it out, it's still in the rack," he said, not looking at me. I walked over to the corner where his printers and scanners were set up and took the pages out of the printing tray. I flipped through them.

"You don't usually take jobs on personally," he said. He was talking about the fact that I'd sent him the details from my home e-mail and not from work.

"I'm working on a search-and-rescue. Ruben thinks he's being funny."

"Nice of you give back to the community once in a while."

"Bite me."

Joel snickered.

"The guy your social security number brought up is called O'Neill," Joel said.

"What?" I walked over to him. O'Neill was a common surname but this kind of coincidence didn't just happen. Not in Westham. Not to me. My life wasn't a novel. I bent over Joel's shoulder and looked at the screen.

"Connor O'Neill, 442 Caldwell, Westham Hills," Joel read out loud. "There's secondary address listed," he said.

My head felt airy. I scrunched the edge of the paper I was holding and it crackled in my fist. "13 Mulberry Street?"

Joel scrolled down.

"Yes, actually... how did you—?"

I held up the papers in my hand. Joel looked at it, and my eyes fell on the screen where the photo attached to his findings opened. The same photo smiled at me from the screen as the one in my hand.

Ruben and Jennifer were after the same guy.

Shit.

Chapter 7

"It's not rocket science. If he's a vampire already, kill him. If he's still human, Ruben can't have him taken out no matter how badly someone wants him. That's just wrong." Joel sipped on his coffee. He'd made us both a cup after I'd kicked over a chair. So I wasn't great at anger management. The last twenty-four hours had made me edgy.

The coffee was bitter and it tasted like he brewed it from a sock, but I sipped mine to be polite.

"It's not like my moral standards have been very high lately," I said.

"True, but you have your reasons." He let those words hang in the air for a while. He knew a bit of what had happened. He didn't know everything. I couldn't bear to live through it long enough to verbalize. I pushed away the fact that he was giving me a reason for my less-than-acceptable behavior. "Besides, you can refuse on legal grounds. Ruben can't say anything about it if it's illegal."

"You know him, Joel. He *will* say something. And with that reporter sniffing around I don't want to look for trouble."

"Reporter?"

"Oh, I didn't say. Some woman is trying to stick her nose into Ruben's business, and by that I don't mean his front."

"Well, that makes it pretty easy then. If it's a human, get out."

"There's something about this reporter that feels wrong. She's too pushy."

"Aren't they always?"

"Only when they know something. And the fact that she does know something that she really shouldn't makes me wonder if she has a better reason than just a story. Something tells me Connor's not human anymore, not if he popped up on our radar."

"You think it's connected?"

I shook my head and gave up on the coffee. "Doubt it, but it's just happening at the same time. Worth noticing. Pity the photo is still human. Without a smell it will make him hard to recognize."

Joel chuckled. "It will be good for you to have a challenge for a change."

I got up and put the half-empty cup of coffee on the table.

"I have to get into the office. I promised Ruben an hour after sundown and I'm already running late."

I rolled out of the garage and started the bike. It came to life with a growl.

"I'll keep you posted," I said, my voice muffled through the helmet, and I turned and opened throttle.

"You're late," Ruben said when I walked into his office. I had my helmet under my arm. I hadn't dropped it on Sonya's desk which meant her mood wasn't fouler than the average. Who said I didn't have grace periods?

"I'm heading out again," I said without answering to his accusation.

"You've got paperwork to look at."

"Not tonight, I have other things on my plate."

Ruben blinked at me, the amber slits of his eyes opening and closing over incredulity.

"Did you just tell me you were too busy to work for me on my time?"

"You sent Lawson to my apartment, Ruben. You can't have your cake and eat it too."

I turned and left his office. His grumbling followed me all the way to the stairwell before it stopped.

I drove to Mulberry Street. The neighborhood was just what I expected it to be. Inconspicuous. The houses were average sized and the all looked almost the same, with nothing that made the one stand out from the other. They all had medium-sized gardens wrapped round them and I guessed if they weren't vampires they would have their standard nine-to-five jobs and two point five children.

Number thirteen was a neat house with white wooden walls and a picket fence. It looked like something from a real estate ad. The windows had green shutters on either side and the garden was in full bloom.

A medley of scents hung in the air. I smelled Jasmine and Lilies, and to the side I spotted an arc covered in white Wisteria that led to the back garden. These were all night flowers. It was the first sign of a vampire house. Anything that could mask their natural smell because they understood the dangers that came with a sharp nose.

I closed my eyes and reached my feelers into the night, looking for people. The street around me had living beings in it, at least half the houses had their people home. But this one was definitely empty. I couldn't feel a thing, no bodies in the house, no smell of blood in the air.

I walked around the back of the house, through the arc and onto a well-manicured lawn. Vampires didn't often take care of their gardens like this. I inspected the windows, and there were no visible changes, no shutters installed. It could be that this house was just a human house with someone who loved gardening.

I pushed my knife underneath a window and slid it open. It creaked a bit but it didn't stick. I slipped in and my lace-ups sank into a plush carpet.

Someone hissed loudly in my ear and I had my Smith & Wesson out in a flash, but at the other end a grey cat had its back arched and claws out. Something. Not Someone. I dared to breathe again. Yellow eyes glared at me.

"You're lucky," I said. I tried to calm my hammering heart. After the night before hissing wasn't my favorite sound. If I'd blown the cat's head off I would have had to worry about blood spatter on everything, and that would have been a real pain in the ass. The cat hissed at me again. This animal obviously didn't like my vampire blood. Another sign that this house might not belong to vampires after all, not if Kitty Galore had a say. The conflicting signs annoyed me.

The house was tidy and it smelled of detergent. I breathed in deeply, trying to find a lead on a smell. It was almost impossible. I'd never come across a vampire that smelled like almost nothing. Humans doused themselves in perfumes and deodorant and it usually pinched my nose. I couldn't tell what I was smelling, and the fact that I was being messed with irritated me even more.

In the bedroom I finally found a scent on the sheets. It was very faint, but it was there. No deodorant had been used to cover it up. I could understand why. With a smell this faint it would take someone a long time to track it, and the deodorant would give it away more than the natural scent at this point.

But it still smelled like vampire, however faint.

The only explanation I could find was that whatever slept here hadn't been in for a while. It was better than admitting I couldn't do everything perfectly.

I walked to the kitchen. The cat sat on the counter, watching. It made a low moaning sound at the back of its throat.

"It's not too late for me to shoot you," I said. It sat next to two bowls, both empty and dry.

"You're master hasn't been here in a while, has he?" I asked. The cat answered with a warning moan.

"Get off it," I said and opened cabinet doors until the scent of cat food wafted out. I poured it into the bowl and filled the other up with water. The cat jumped up next to me, ignoring my presence, and dived into the food. By the looks of things it was hungry. I didn't reach out to stroke it, it would only try to scratch me anyway. But it was kind of nice seeing something alive be grateful for something I'd done, and not dead or resenting.

Maybe I should get myself a pet.

The front door clicked and the sound travelled through my bones. I stepped back, melting into the darkness. I pushed myself up against a tall cabinet and took out my Smith & Wesson. With my other hand I felt for the stake at my hip. If this guy was a vampire, the one I was looking for, he was going to get it. Nothing like a surprise attack at home.

"Hey, Clyde," a deep voice said. It was husky and silky, and it was like music to listen to. It sent shivers down my spine in a warm way, not the foreboding kind I usually felt. I wondered vaguely what had happened to Bonnie if this cat was Clyde.

"Sorry I disappeared for a while." The cast answered with soft mewing sounds.

I couldn't see the guy, but I heard him move towards the kitchen. Then the movement stopped.

"Who fed you?" he asked, alarm in his voice. He was close enough for me to smell, and I took a deep breath, letting the smell into my nostrils, my mind racing to place it. Definitely vampire. Warm blood, mutated cells. I was betting on fangs. With it was a strong pull, lacing all the signals. I didn't usually feel this drawn to something. I took two seconds to puzzle over it, but then I pushed it away. There was one way to break a magnetic pull – eliminate the source.

I stepped out from behind the cabinet, pointing my S&W right at his face. He was shocked. I could feel it in the air. But strangely there was no fear. Usually it dominated. There wasn't even a trace. In the dim lighting I could see his hands lift up, a surrender.

His hair was a pale blond in the light falling in through the window. He looked a lot like the photo in the dark, save for the ghostly pale skin and the elongated limbs.

"Mr. O'Neill," I said. It wasn't a question.

"What do you want?" he asked. He didn't try to fight or run. But still, the smell of vampire became stronger. It was almost as if he could hide it, and he was letting up now. Was that possible? I'd never met a vampire that could pretend to be human.

I heard him take a long, slow breath. He was smelling me, too. It was a predator thing. We weren't two people, facing off. We were animals. But this wasn't going to be a fight for dominance like they do it in the animal word. With a gun like mine we both knew who was boss. My finger curled around the trigger. If I couldn't get in close enough for a stake, I was going to shoot.

"I know you," he said. The words caught me off guard and I let go of the trigger. He'd been about one squeeze away from death. I stepped to the side, gun still pointing at his face, and got the light.

The yellow light flooded the room, brightening the white tiles to a glare. My eyes adjusted quickly, but he held up his arms over his eyes to shield it. Vampire eyes were sensitive even to man-made light. He grimaced and I spotted fangs touching his bottom lip.

"What do you know about me?" I demanded.

"Your smell," he said. His voice was trembling a little, and it made me wonder if he really wasn't scared, or if he'd managed to mask his fear as well. "Your scent, I've smelled it before."

He slowly dropped his arms, and the vampire I'd saved that morning in the alley stood in front of me. His neck wounds were healed up and he didn't have the dark circles under his eyes anymore, but it was definitely him. Something in my body lurked and I silently scolded my weakness. The attraction was ridiculous.

"Connor?" I asked, just to be sure. He nodded.

In a flash I had him up against the wall, with my forearm against his throat. He gasped and squirmed underneath my grip. I didn't have my chain on me, I'd left it with the bike. Dammit. I hadn't expected to catch one home. If he dematerialized now I would lose him.

"What are you?" he asked in a hoarse voice. Despite his strong ability to disguise himself his naivety showed through. He didn't know a half-breed when he saw one. I'd moved in a blur like him, I was strong like him. But when I spoke I knew he noticed my blunt teeth. His eyes were on my mouth. It let my eyes trail down to his too. His fangs were sharp, resting lightly on his bottom lip. His lips were smooth and full but not too thick for a man. I forced my eyes back onto his.

"There's a warrant out for you," I said. Maybe only police spoke about warrants. Maybe bad guys called it something else. I didn't know.

"Dead or alive?"

"Dead."

I positioned the stake underneath his ribs. I looked up into his eyes. They were dark blue, deep like the ocean. I could fall into them if I wasn't careful. I swallowed hard. We were frozen like that, with me half-choking him, and time stood still. I felt something around us, not the mist I'd expected but a shift in the atmosphere. It became so thick I was sure I could run my fingers through it. I frowned and slowly released him, letting him stand on his own two feet.

He didn't run or fight or try to dematerialize. Instead he stood there, looking at me while I was gaping at him.

He lifted his hand slowly, and I flinched when he brought it closer, but I didn't move away. His fingers touched the skin above my right eyebrow and he brushed my hair out of my face. A warm surge of electricity raced through my body. My blood hummed in my veins.

"You're bruised," he said, and I remembered what I must look like.

"It happens," I said and regretted justifying it. Who was he?

"I woke up in a garage and your scent hung around me like fog," Connor said. His fingers were still in my hair. I had to step away. Actually, I had to stake the vampire. I was aware of the tips of teeth, visible when he spoke. But the way he combed the tips of his fingers through my hair was nice. It made me feel warm. When last had I felt warm? And his eyes, I couldn't look into his eyes and kill him. They hypnotized me and I wanted to keep staring into them.

"You were in the alley," I said, and my voice was husky, not my own. "The sun was coming up."

"You saved me then to kill me now?"

"It's my job," I said and looked away so his eyes wouldn't make me betray myself even further.

"What's stopping you?"

"You," I whispered before I could stop myself.

Something changed in Connor's eyes. An emotion flickered across his face, too fast for me to read. I became aware of the cat, purring on the counter like a tractor. This one liked vampires, apparently. It was reveling in Connor's presence.

So it was just me it hated. Nice to know.

A sound outside ripped us out of the spell we were caught in. Connor cocked his head and listened. Even with my half-breed ears I was going to miss sounds a vampire could hear. I didn't have all of it, just most of it.

"Something tells me I'm not the only person after you," I said. He shook his head. If the security he set up around his information online was anything to go by, he had much more on his plate than I did.

"You're not safe if you stay here, either. At the moment I'm just using this house as a distraction."

"And you're leaving your cat behind to fend for itself?"

He glanced at me. "For someone who kills people that's a very judgmental statement."

His words were sharp and I felt my insides cringe away like he'd physically done something to me. I shook my head. Who the hell was he? I didn't care what he thought. I wouldn't.

"So you want to tell me who's out to kill you?"

"Are you planning on eliminating competition? Because that would be swell." He moved around the kitchen, turning his head to catch sounds of the night. Twice he sniffed the air. Half the time he looked like he didn't know what was going on, and the other half he looked like he'd been a vampire for years.

"You've been spending a lot of time with vampires," I said, suddenly realizing what I was seeing. He nodded slowly.

"I had a couple work in my firm with me, until I found out they were dealing with illegal things behind my back. When I fired them things turned ugly, so I turned vampire."

"You chose to turn?" It sounded appalling. I couldn't imagine giving up something as perfect as humanity for something as raw and emotionless and being a vampire.

"It's survival. You know better than any that a vampire is difficult to kill, where a human can just be taken out. I wasn't my time to go."

"Your fiancée is looking for you," I said. The atmosphere changed again, it suddenly became ice cold, like someone had just switched off the heat.

"You know Jennifer?" he asked.

"She's the one that hired me."

"To kill me?" he looked confused.

"Not if you were human. Vampire puts you on my kill list."

Connor looked like he thought about it for a moment. I could see cogs turning behind his eyes, but his face was carefully blank.

"You're fun," he said in a dull voice and I figured he'd finally come to his conclusions. They were the right ones, too, if he was being sarcastic with me. At the end of the day people weren't nice to me when they understood what I did.

I opened my mouth to say something but he held up his hand, listening.

"I have to go, trouble's coming," he said, and then he disappeared. It was almost like he'd dissolved at record speed, and the feel of him lingered a short while after he'd dematerialized. I took a deep breath and tried to swallow, but my mouth was dry and my throat felt like sandpaper. The words I'd wanted to speak still rolled around on my tongue, and I stood alone in the kitchen, trying to decide which way was up in my life.

"Oh, you're in trouble now," I said to myself. This was the first mark that had gotten away from me, not because it had outsmarted me, but because I'd been rendered dumb. I felt like a fool. Anger bubbled up in my throat, and my blood heated up beneath my skin. Damn vampires. Damn Connor. Damn my stupid life. I hated all the killing, hated that I needed it to survive. And the same time I hated myself for letting one get away.

Clyde hissed at me, mouth open and teeth bare. I didn't have fangs, but I could hold my own in a cat fight. I hissed right back. The cat arched its back and squealed, and then disappeared down the passage.

I left the house, before the Conner's troubles caught up to me, too.

Chapter 8

Sonya's desk was empty when I reached the office half an hour before sunrise. The days rolling over from one to another when I finished work still affected me. It made me feel time was getting away from me. It was heading onto Thursday. I had been at this for almost a week and had nothing to show for it.

"Your secretary is missing," I said to Ruben, walking into his office without an announcement.

"She's wasn't feeling well. I let her off early."

"Big of you."

I dropped three sets of keys and ID cards on Ruben's desk. He frowned at my hand. I had blood across my fingers and under my nails, and it stained the rim of my sleeve as well, although it was harder to see against the black leather.

"Busy night?" he asked. I shrugged.

After I'd left Connor's place I'd gone on a rampage. I'd killed all the orders I'd received from Ruben. I'd had to feel like I was still good for something, like I had some sort of worth. I'd stood face to face with one of my marks and I hadn't been able to kill him.

Didn't want to, I corrected myself. I could still do it. I wasn't getting weak. I wouldn't let myself come to that point.

"What are these?" Ruben asked, frowning at the three cards he'd arranged in front of him in a row.

"Kills," I said. Obviously. "I don't exactly take them to coffee."

He looked up at me, his eyes almost-yellow, annoyed.

"These are low level, Adele. I told you, you need to prioritize that last one I gave you. I've got clients on my case about it."

I shifted my weight from one foot to the other and looked out the window. The sky was changing, the darkness incomplete now with the warning of dawn.

"I'm still tracking him. I haven't found a solid lead." I didn't want him to know I'd failed with Connor. I didn't want him to know that I saw Connor as a *he* and not an *it* even though he was a vampire. I didn't want Ruben to know that I referred to him as Connor.

"You're getting sloppy, Adele. You're usually on top of them in one night."

"You just gave me a social security number. What do you expect from me?"

He looked at me and I looked right back, locking us in a stare-down. In Ruben's world it was a warning. Human's did it to emphasize their point, their resolve. They did it to win an argument.

In my world it was a fight for dominance. If one predator locked eyes with another it was a challenge. And Ruben sure as shit didn't want to challenge me. I had a lot more on him, speed and strength and two guns and a knife. He was going to end up very far second.

Ruben broke the stare and looked down at the ID cards again. He didn't realize he'd just lost the fight. I was the Alpha between me and him, no matter who paid who at the end of the month.

"Just make sure you get this over and done with," he said, not looking at me. "Talk to your friends, call your contacts. I know you run to a techy when you need something. Now would be a good time to do that."

The way he said it got my back up. I didn't *run* to anyone.

"I said I would get it done," I said, and my voice was hard and cold as ice. Ruben glanced up at me. I didn't know what my face showed, but he nodded.

"You better," he said but his voice was empty of the warning his words were suggesting.

I drove home and put away my guns, stripping out of my leather and getting into the shower. I scrubbed my skin until it was raw. The thing about blood was that once it was dried it was damn hard to get off. I didn't want to arrive at my training with blood on my hands. Much less at Aspen's.

By the time I was ready to leave again it was already heading on towards eight o'clock. I picked up my phone and dialed her number, but only got through to voicemail.

"I've got training until ten today, I'll stop by afterward. Keep something warm for me, Sensei is going to make sure I'm starving."

I hopped on my bike and drove into town. It was faster than any public transport system was going to get me to the Academy.

I met with Sensei an hour earlier to make up for missing my session yesterday. We started with a warm-up and then some sparring. Everything went well until he knocked me in the head. If I was fine nothing would have happened, I would have recovered and went after him for it. But my head hurt more than I'd expected it would, and I sprawled on the floor. I held my hand up for him to just to wait a second. I didn't have to say anything, he put two and two together.

"Either you're running with the wrong crowd, or my teaching isn't working. What happened?"

"I stepped into the wrong territory, is all," I answered. Sensei looked at me until I squirmed under his stare.

"Really, it was nothing. You should see the other guy." I chuckled half-heartedly. Of course it hadn't been another guy. It had been a woman. And I hadn't made a mark on her save for the burn I was sure she carried on her leg now after I'd cut her with my silver blade. But I wasn't going to admit any of that to Sensei. Besides, he didn't know about all the other injuries.

"I'm starting to think I should be worried about you on more than just a self-defense and fighting-technique level," he said, starting with the stretching routine I mirrored for warm-up.

"Don't worry about it," I said. "I can handle myself."

"Doesn't sound like it," he said. I steeled myself against the insult. I would show him in our sparring and hand-to-hand just now. I could still put him on his back and make him hurt. I ignored that it was because he was only a human, and my enemies almost never were.

At the back of my mind I wondered if I would be able to find a vampire that would train me in supernatural fighting skills. It might have come in handier than what I was doing now. That of course meant that I would have to know a vampire without killing it. And that wasn't something I liked to do. Not because I killed every vampire I knew, but because I only spoke to them when I was about to kill them. It was a strange, backward cycle.

And in the middle of it all, holding everything together like a stake in the middle, was Connor. The one vampire I hadn't managed to kill. The one vampire I didn't even really hate, if I had to admit it. I shook my head. I wasn't going to admit it, just yet. There was still time. Hatred was better when it was left simmering for a while.

"You're not doing this for fun, are you?" Sensei asked me when I all but crawled to my bag and fished out my water bottle. I'd taken it all out on him, and he looked like he'd just had a warm-up. Maybe he had energy left because he wasn't beating himself up on top of everything.

"I don't—"

"You know, your stories are getting old," he said and walked over to the chair next to my bag, sitting down. "All I'm seeing is you getting hurt, and then coming down here to take whatever you're mad about out on me. I don't mind being a punching bag, that's my job. But just hitting everything and everyone you see isn't going to fix whatever's bothering you."

"It's worked for me so far," I lied. The truth was it wasn't working at all. But what else could I do? Forgiveness wasn't an option, and it sounded ridiculous to scale down to a nine-to-five desk job now.

I threw my things in my bag without ceremony. When I wanted to stand up Sensei put his hand on my shoulder. The warmth of his touch made my want to lean into it and to cringe away all at the same time. Instead I just froze. My muscles were tense. I could take him again if I had to.

I shook my head to get the thoughts out. This wasn't an attack. Not everything was.

"I don't know what you're doing. But you've been coming here for long enough with the same routine... all I'm saying is that not everyone is an enemy. There are the few in your life who are willing to be your friends."

He stood up and walked away from me without a care in a world, like he always did. I resented that. He could walk away and take on his next student without the darkness trying to catch up with him, and I walked out of the door into the past.

I reached Aspen's house half an hour after my training session. Every muscle in my body felt numb and complained when I slid off my bike. Zelda opened the front door when she heard my bike's engine.

"Adele," she exclaimed, looking at the motorcycle over my shoulder when I walked toward the front porch. "You don't usually come here on that."

"I had a change in routine today. I left her a voicemail," I answered. When I was on the steps, Zelda shook her head.

"Aspen's gone out."

I froze in my tracks, one leg still hovering in the air over the last step. I put it down again without climbing further.

"Out where?"

"She went shopping. Claude took her about..." she lifted her wrist and squinted at her watch. "... an hour ago."

I swore under my breath in a way that was very unbecoming for a lady.

"How could you just let her go?"

"Because I'm her nurse not her warden," she said matter-of-factly. "Claude is with her."

"Claude is a damn *driver*." I sneered and spun around, running for my bike. Zelda called after me, but I didn't hear what she was saying. I was already pushing the helmet over my head and I had the bike started and reeling down the road in a flash.

I was overreacting. I knew I was. But it had been a hell of a week and if someone was on my case and knew what I was, how was she safe? My heart hammered in my chest and I struggled to breathe. Shopping wasn't a bad thing, was it? Aspen was a grown woman. But she was also half-vampire, and with her teeth she looked pretty mythical. And she was in a wheelchair.

What if someone decided they didn't like her? If they accidentally saw her teeth even when she knew how to smile and speak to conceal them? She was so vulnerable. If something happened to her and I couldn't save her... it would all be my fault. Again.

I shook my head while I flew towards the mall. I tried to get rid of the images that flashed in my mind's eye. Aspen had just been a teenager when her whole life had been ripped apart. She'd only had me, and even then I hadn't been able to save her from a life that was worse than death.

I pulled into a parking space for motorcycles and ran into the mall. I dialed Aspen's number in the run and to my relief it rang.

"Adele," her clear voice rang over the speaker.

"Where are you?" I asked.

"I'm at the mall. I'm shopping."

"I mean what shop? Let me come find you." I swallowed the excess spit in my mouth from running.

"You're here? I'm at the food court."

I hung up and made my way to the food court. The mall was busy this time of the morning, and I pushed my way through bustling groups of people. Finally I spotted her at a table with the chair removed for her wheel chair, drinking a soda.

"What are you doing here?" she asked when I collapsed on a chair next to her and tried to catch my breath. The air came in ragged gasps and burned my lungs on the way in and out. No matter how fit I was, the kind of fear I kindled about Aspen got me breathless and heaving every time.

"I just wanted to say hello," I lied.

Aspen narrowed her eyes at me. "You're checking up on me."

"I'm not. I just... Shit Aspen. What if something happened to you?"

Aspen sighed and put down her soda with a clunk. "Don't you think you're being a bit much?" she asked. I knew I was but I wasn't going to admit to it. "I'm just shopping. I'm allowed to get out of the house and have a life, you know."

I nodded, looking around the food court, scanning for anything that might look like trouble.

"Claude is here to help me," she said and nodded toward the burger stand where I saw the driver standing in line. "And besides, what's going to happen to me? The worst already had and I survived it."

I looked down at her wheelchair and her words snapped around me like whips.

"I'm sorry," I said, even though I wasn't. The only thing I regretted was that she felt I was being over-protective. I wasn't sorry at all for the fact that I *was* overprotective. I just needed her safe. I wasn't going to let her get hurt again, even if it killed me.

I offered her a smile that she returned after a moment of hesitation. "Well, after that episode, I think I'm going to head home and have a shower. I'm still sweaty from training."

Aspen nodded. "I'll see you tomorrow. And don't worry about me, okay? I'm perfectly fine."

"Okay," I said, trying to sound confident about it. I turned and walked away.

I'd almost reached my bike when my phone rang. I pulled it out and looked at the caller ID. It was Joel.

"Can I come over?" he asked. Joel never came over to my place. No one did. I didn't like showing people the dump I lived in.

"I'm still out. Let me come to you. I'll be there in ten."

"No, don't do that," he said and his voice sounded panicky. "Stay where you are, I'll come to you."

"What's going on?"

"Someone trashed my place. I have footage, and I think you need to see this."

I arranged for him to meet me at the mall, at a coffee shop on the other side so I wouldn't run into Aspen and make her think I was keeping an eye on her. I put my helmet back on my bike, and weaved my way into the crowds again. My eyes felt gritty when I blinked and my head thumped dully. I was running on eighteen hours with no sleep, and with sleeping in yesterday morning and training twice as hard today my clock was off and my body complained.

I found the coffee shop we'd agreed on and found a table in the back where the hum of voices all around us could drown out conversation. I texted Joel where to find me, and leaned back, waiting. I hated being out in public like this. There were people around me everywhere, groups of three laughing, couples staring into each other's eyes... it was all very normal.

In my nighttime career of murder and mayhem it was difficult to remember a day time life that looked so ordinary. I wondered what my life would have looked like if I didn't have Aspen to worry about. If my mother was still alive. If my father wasn't locked up in a metal cell with no light so he wouldn't fry or dematerialize.

Joel arrived just in time to snap me out of the spiral my thoughts were pulling me into.

"I'm glad you're here," he said, sitting down. He looked about as panicked as I had felt a half hour earlier. He looked at me, and then let his eyes slide down and back up my body.

"You look different."

I rolled my eyes. "Don't remind me."

"No, it looks good. The whole I-actually-do-have-a-heart look works on you."

I punched him lightly on the shoulder and he leaned back in his chair, ducking away from me.

"I'm not here for insults," I said.

"Only you would take a compliment as an insult. If I told you you look like a serial killer, I might get you to smile. You're all backwards, Adele."

"Are we here to discuss you, or me?" I asked irritably.

"You're right," he said. "Well, someone got into the pit and trashed everything. All my computers are ruined. When I got there this morning it looked like a hurricane had been through it, all my papers were scattered. It's a hell of a lot of money in damages, too."

"I didn't know people knew about your work place," I said. Joel was discreet in his dealings.

"Only three people do, and you and I are two of them."

"You said you have footage?"

He nodded and produced a laptop bag that I hadn't noticed him carrying over his shoulder.

"This one's fine, though," I said, nodding at the laptop.

"I keep this one on me. It has all my cameras linked up to it."

I didn't know Joel had cameras everywhere. I hadn't noticed any, and for me that's saying something.

"They're thumb-tack cameras," Joel said as if he'd read my mind. "No one's supposed to see them. I invented them myself." He said it like he wanted a pat on the back. He wasn't going to get it from me.

"Do you have more where those came from?" I asked instead. He nodded, a smile slowly creeping across his face. "I could do with some surveillance at my place." It was a compliment if I wanted some too. "Maybe Aspen's as well," I added.

"I won't be able to set it up for you straight away, I have to sort out the pit first and find them. I also need to check your system to see if it's up to date enough to run them."

I thought back to my computer. Unlikely, but maybe Joel could do a bit of magic.

"Pity you can't do it soon. I have a feeling someone's on my trail."

Joel flipped open his laptop. He pulled up a screen split four-ways and a black and white tape showed the pit. Someone in black clothes appeared and started ransacking the place, throwing over tables, kicking monitors and cabinets over.

"What was he looking for?"

"Not he, she," Joel said, and the next frame showed the person from the side. It was clearly a woman, and she had white hair. She wore a bandana over her mouth so it was impossible to see her face properly, but I was pretty sure I knew her.

"How did she know we were linked?" I asked.

"It's her, isn't it?" Joel asked. "I knew it was."

"What did she want?"

"I don't know. As far as I can tell nothing's missing. Just destroyed. More like a warning than a hit."

I took a deep breath and blew it out again. A warning I could believe. A hit would have been death. I was pretty sure that even the other night's attack on me had been more of a warning. I knew how I fought to the death. I doubted she would have fled from an unfinished job.

"I'm going to have to find her and put an end to this nonsense." It was one thing if I got beaten up. It was different when the people I cared about were thrown in the mix.

"Don't plan your revenge just yet," Joel said. "I get all the information my servers find sent to the laptop. Back-ups and all that. This came through just before the system went offline."

He clicked on a tab at the bottom of the screen and pulled up a website address. The newspaper article appeared on screen.

Connor O'Neill, king of Westham's Business District and part of Westham's

social elite went missing after a troubling report came to light that suggested he

is involved in Vampire Trafficking. Connor O'Neill, third generational owner

of O'Neill & Grodin Inc. was one of the forerunners for vampire-human

equality and backed this by employing vampires. O'Neill & Grodin Inc. was

one of the first companies to implement this employment structure with many

other companies following suit. To date his company employees are 30% vampire

which ranks as one of the highest in the country.

Questions are being raised by partners and stockholders whether the vampire

employment was a cover, where some are going as far as saying that O'Neill used

it as a front to attract vampires which he then shipped off to work in illegal

blood-banks in the middle-east.

Vampire trafficking is a relatively new concept and there is a fresh market for it,

where vampires are used for anything from scientific experimenting and the search

for a viable antidote to 'cure' vampirism, to fetishes and fantasies. With the life expectancy being so high, and vampires' ability to heal so fast, they are sold at an

extremely high price.

Chief of Police Sorrel Marx comments: "O'Neill has always been a big name in

Westham and it's difficult to believe he's behind something this horrendous, but

we've been surprised before. The police are working day and night to solve this.

Vampires are new to society but we will fight to protect their rights just as we would

for humans." The case is still being investigated. Jennifer Lawson, O'Neill's fiancée,

has no comment on the topic but she's been questioned by police about her

involvement and she continues to be under public scrutiny.

I frowned and read the article again.

"Looks like your mark is in a lot of trouble."

"He said he had to change to get out of it," I mumbled, more to myself than to Joel, but he'd heard me.

"He what? You spoke to him?"

I closed my eyes for a moment and scolded myself for slipping up.

"I ran into him when I was searching his house," I said. I wasn't going to lie to Joel. There might have been times where I didn't tell him the whole truth, but I wouldn't lie to him.

"How much did you get out of him before you killed him?"

"No enough," I said. I hadn't killed him, of course, but that counted as omission of truth. Besides, I should have asked more questions. And after this, I would if I saw him again. If I could control myself to not kill him right away.

Right.

"Was this in the newspapers?" I asked.

Joel nodded. I didn't read the papers, but then again, neither did Joel.

"Someone's been lying to me." I thought back to the conversation with Jennifer. It must have been convenient to her that I didn't know about the whole scandal. I would have a word with her, too.

"Who wrote this?" I asked, a thought suddenly dawning on me. Joel scrolled down, squinting at the screen.

"A Celia Clemens," he said.

Clemens. It sounded familiar. A name I could trace besides Jennifer and Connor.

"Thanks for this," I said to Joel, getting up. "And I'm sorry about your place. I'll sort it out."

"You just worry about your face. If she could do that to my hardware I'd hate to know what she'll do to someone that bleeds.

Chapter 9

I left the mall feeling frustrated and tired, and that made me grumpy. I tore down the road, speeding tickets to hell. My head spun with information and my fingers itched for some action. I hadn't slept yet before my last set of kills, but I needed to get this poison out of my system.

I hated being the one that wasn't on top of things. I hated being on the bottom rung of the game. And this woman, whoever she was, was messing with my people. And with me.

And on top of that, Connor and vampire trafficking? I had no kind of loyalty to vampires, I was a killer for crying out loud. But trafficking? That just seemed wrong. The whole idea of life stretching to infinity and laced with torture made me feel uncomfortable. I shook my head, my view of the road shaking in my helmet. I had to get my mind straight. I couldn't pick and choose. I couldn't hate them and protect them at the same time.

But what did I feel, then? Why did this news upset me so much? It felt like a stake, lodged under my ribs and it moved painfully around every time I moved, every time I breathed. This was why I had to kill him. This was why it had been such a carnal mistake that I'd let him go. Everyone had flaws. Being half vampire, or even completely, was the least of it, it seemed.

I thought suddenly of Jennifer. How much had she known about it? How much had she been involved with? Giving the police a story was one thing. I was starting to wonder about her motivation to find him. I was pissed she'd lied to me. People didn't just lie to me and get away with it. Was it to give him up? Or was it to save him and by definition save herself?

My head spun with all the questions and thoughts, and by the time I got home the only thing that I permitted to keep rolling around my mind was the fact that my people were being messed with, and someone had to pay.

Who would have guessed I was a territorial animal? For someone who passed as human I was a wild and possessive. Go figure.

I fell into bed, but not before I reloaded the Glock under my pillow with new ammunition, and slid the Smith & Wesson under my bed instead of returning it to my gun safe. Nervous much? The fact was that if I woke up with a blond bitch hovering over my face I wanted to end it with the least amount of effort. I was done playing games. I was never one to toe the line. I just stepped over the damn thing and started shooting.

I woke up to three messages on my phone and a handful of missed calls from private numbers. None of them were from Aspen, and that was enough for me to relax.

Ruben had tried to get a hold of me. I dialed his cell.

"Anxious to see me?" I asked when he picked up on the first ring.

"I want to make sure you're getting your ass in here the moment the sun goes down and taking care of business. I want this finished."

"You sound like someone's chewing your ass."

He took a deep breath and I knew it was to calm down before he broke something on his end of the line. The downside of violence was that it was no fun when it wasn't in person. "You have no idea what's at stake here."

"A lot of cash?

He chuckled without emotion. "If it were only that easy. Your life is simple enough. You pull a trigger and you troubles are over. I have mine live long enough to come back and bite me."

"I'll be there," I said and hung up. My life was easy, was it? Because I could just shoot my troubles and go to bed without a headache.

If only it were that easy. The problem with killing was that those really did come back to haunt you, no matter how justified. And there had been plenty reasons for me to pick up a gun in the first place. But it was safer to let Ruben believe that his life was difficult, cocooned in the safety of his office while I got blood on my hands. There were some things that couldn't be repaid otherwise, even if it meant returning it in death.

I got dressed in my leathers and looked at myself in the mirror. I tried not to do it. I looked as deadly as my father, with my dark hair and haunted eyes. I curled my lips back for the confirmation that I was only looking at myself. No fangs. No threat. I shuddered and shrugged into my holsters. The guns against my body were a kind of security. It was something I understood, something solid. A gun was something I could trust. It didn't pretend that it of loved me when all it could offer was death.

It hardly ever misfired, so the pull of a trigger was a sure fire way of doing the right kind of damage, and it was heavy and grounded the way trust should be.

I looked at the clock. It was still early. The sun cast a fiery glow through my window. I walked out the door anyway, and got on my bike. I switched it on and let it idle, letting my thoughts go. I twisted the throttle and pulled out into the street, with the intention of driving around until it was time to head to the office.

Instead, I ended up in front of Westham Penitentiary. The big grey building sat squat, like it had sunken in on itself with the weight of its content. It was divided up into two sides, the one half reinforced with metal within the walls and no windows to keep mythical creatures in and guards had silver bullets. The visitor queues shifted from the human building during the day to the vampire building at night. The realization of where my body had taken me when my mind was occupied swirled like nausea in my stomach.

I walked inside and went through the motions, filling out the forms and producing my ID. Eventually I sat in the uncomfortable plastic chair with the thick glass in front of me. I shivered and my chest felt like lead. Suddenly I wanted to run, but just as I motioned to get up, he walked through the door.

He wore an orange jumpsuit and his black hair was almost completely grey now. He looked like he hadn't shaved in a couple of days. But it was what was under the hair and clothes that scared me. My father looked like he had doubled in age. His face sagged and his cheeks were sunken, his blue irises watered down so much it was difficult to tell what color they had been once. And at the same time the face that stared back at me was still the face of the father I'd grown up with. And still the monster I hated.

He picked up the phone attached to the partition, and held it against his ear. I did the same. The receiver was cold and heavy against my cheek.

"I didn't expect to see you," my dad said.

"I didn't expect to come."

A silence hung between us filled with everything we couldn't say.

"How's Aspen?"

"She's doing alright," I answered stiffly. No thanks to you, I added silently. "I'm doing well too, thank you for asking."

He looked at me and he didn't need to say the words. I could hear them anyway. I didn't look like I was doing okay. I didn't feel like it either.

His eyes glazed over and he looked passed me at a memory that transported him to a different world. I guessed that in a place as colorless and drab as this, he had to escape to a world he'd created himself. He'd gotten good at it. I know I had, and my prison wasn't even something tangible.

"I never meant to do any of it," he said so softly I could barely make out the words. But what he said wasn't lost on me.

"Bit late for that now..."

"I miss her." He rubbed his eyes like he was wiping away tears, but when he looked at me there was no trace of crying. There was no question about where Aspen had gotten that skill. I wondered who *she* was. The mother I lost or the sister I was fighting to keep. He'd lost both even when it wasn't a straight kill the second time round. Goose bumps stretched over my body like a duvet, stuffed with the memories of times past and loved ones lost, rather than the feather of geese.

"Will you ask Aspen to come see me?" he asked.

"You're the last person on this earth she wants to see, dad. Besides, the jailhouse isn't exactly wheelchair friendly." He flinched at my remark. I wondered how much he refused to acknowledge.

"I..." his face was a blank mask, his lips moving without a sound. It was enough quiet space for me to spill my own bitterness into the silence.

"You remember that, don't you? Why you're here? Mom's dead, and Aspen is crippled for the rest of her life. And I'm left behind fixing every mistake you made because you weren't enough of a man to do it yourself."

My dad looked down at his hand on the plastic table in front of him. He picked at his forefinger nail with his thumb. He hummed a wilting tune, and I wondered for a moment if he was sane at all. Maybe it would have been easier to accept if he'd been declared clinically insane. If a crazy had made those decisions I could forgive them somehow – a lapse in judgment, a lapse in who my father really was – but the fact was that none of that was what had happened. During the court case two psychologists had visited with him and both had declared him more sane than most of the people that walked the streets. If anything, the insanity was creeping in now, with the absence of the real world to keep him in check.

"Why are you here?" he suddenly asked, looking at me, and it was the sharpest I'd seen his eyes in years. I looked at him for a long time before I answered him.

"I don't know. I never really know why I end up coming to see you." No matter how many kills I made, I knew that the man I really wanted dead was still here. Maybe one day I could lay down my guns, but there were too many vampires out there, too many people that could still be killed. Too many Aspens in this world, and not enough Adeles.

"Maybe it's because every time you walk out of those doors I hope that I can see a different person. Someone who hadn't done all those things. But every time it's just you coming through that door."

"Just me," he echoed.

I put down the phone and stood up. I was running late for work. I shouldn't have come in the first place. I never knew why I ended up here of all places. I never knew why I kept running back to the one man I truly hated, in the most raw sense of the word. It was his face I saw every time a forced my stake into a vampire heart, or pulled a trigger. It was his blood I saw splattered on the walls behind the victims, on my hands after a long night. In my nightmares.

I looked over my shoulder. An officer was already leading him away from the booth, but his eyes locked with mine and his lips were moving. 'I love you' he mouthed.

I turned my back and kept walking.

In the parking lot I sat on my bike. The last fingers of sunshine dragged across the horizon, leaving stretched shadows behind like scars. I felt ripped apart, like there was a gaping hole in my chest and everything I breathed in just escaped through it again. I gasped for air, fighting down the lump that rose in my throat.

"Are you alright?" I heard a voice behind me. I swallowed my emotions and turned around. My hand was already on the knife on my thigh.

Connor stood half behind me, and he looked concerned. Something inside me jumped and I tried to place what I was feeling. I looked toward the horizon again, and noticed the last light was gone. What remained now was just an afterthought.

"You're out early," I said, not answering his question. "It's a big risk for a pure bred to be out this close to sunset."

"A pure bred?"

I bit my tongue. By mentioning pure bred I was suggesting that there was a breed that wasn't pure. I shook my head.

"What are you doing here?" he asked.

"I guess I could ask you the same thing."

"You avoid all my questions," he pointed out. "I have unfinished business I need to tie up." He sighed and he looked so sad for a moment that I wondered if it was my job to do something about it. Was someone going to take care of mine? We all had to deal with our own troubles. The emotion cleared as quickly as it had arrived, and his face was carefully expressionless. "When you join the dark side you don't realize how many ends you can't seem to tie up. Even if none of it was your choice in the first place."

"As opposed to the darkness you created in you past life?" I asked. Connor blanched, if that was possible for a vampire whose skin was already too pale.

"So you've heard," he said.

"Anyone who reads papers knows."

"Except you didn't read papers. It was like talking to a long lost friend when I realized you didn't know. You're only hunting me as a job aren't you?"

I shrugged. Admitting to that made it sound worse than it was, in my opinion. I didn't need to be classified in the same group as him.

"I'm guessing you have interest in there," he said, gesturing his head toward the building. "Vampire?"

I stilled. "How did you guess?"

"The entrance to the human facility is on the other side." He smiled a brilliant smile that flashed long white teeth. He would still learn to hide those in public. "I didn't peg you for the vampire-loving type. What with you trying to stake me and all."

"I'm not," I said flatly. Speaking of staking, for someone who knew for a fact I'd intended to kill him he was being very casual around me.

"So, are all those stories true?" I wanted to stop myself, but I had to ask. It was about the vampires. I told myself that it was about them, about their lives. I didn't want to admit to myself that it was also about Connor. That I didn't want to be disappointed in him.

"Would it make a difference to you if it were? Weren't you going to kill me anyway?"

I looked down at my hands. I didn't know the answer to that question, and that pissed me off.

"You don't seem too worried about it," I said instead. "The fact that the reason you know me at all is because I was about to kill you."

"But you didn't."

He shrugged and jammed his hands into his pockets. He wore civilian clothes, and if it weren't for the small telltale signs and the obvious fangs, I would say he could pass for human. His ability to disguise himself was amusing. I hadn't met a vampire that could do that. For that matter I haven't really given any of them a chance.

"I don't know, maybe I like you," he said and his words knocked whatever I was thinking out of my head.

"You go for the hard-asses, do you? Handsome man like you? What would Jennifer say?"

His face turned to stone, his lips set in a straight line. "She's not really the kind of person that fits into this world," he said.

"Are you talking about the trafficking world, or the vampire one?"

He looked at me for a long time. When he finally spoke it wasn't to answer my question. We were playing the same game.

He looked down at his shoes. "In another life... Sometimes it takes nearly dying to realize how much time you were wasting on the wrong stuff, and how many people you dedicated yourself to for the wrong reasons."

I groaned. "I don't do sagas," I said. I hated it when people, or vampires in this case, got all emotional on me. It was just something I didn't do. Emotion was for weaklings. I'd worked hard to push mine far enough away to believe it didn't exist. I really would have appreciated it if others could do the same.

Connor chuckled. "I want to see you again."

"See me again?" I echoed because I couldn't remember any of our meeting where I hadn't tried to kill him, so it seemed strange. Maybe he wanted a challenge.

"Yeah. Saturday."

"In the day?"

He shrugged again. "Nighttime would suit me better." Obviously, I was being stupid. He looked toward the horizon, and then toward jail. "I have to get going," he said. "One of my friends was locked up for trafficking. Imagine that."

"Won't they be looking out for you?"

"It's hard to find someone when they're not what you expect."

I smiled despite myself. "I'll see you after sunset on Saturday. You have some explaining to do if I want to take my job seriously."

"That sounds a lot like a compromise to me. I didn't think you did that often."

"Never," I agreed.

"Promise to leave the stake behind?"

I nodded. He didn't say anything about knives and guns.

Connor started fading, see-through, when he spoke one more sentence.

"For what it's worth, I didn't do it. Some people I hired did. When I found out I had to save myself. You can fill in the blanks for yourself." He dematerialized and I was left alone again, cursing myself for being an idiot. For feeling the emptiness he'd left behind.

It was okay, I reassured myself. I needed to know who was after him and why. That was why I'd agreed. Of course. When I drove toward the office I kept repeating it to myself, like a mantra. Maybe if I did it often enough, I would start believing it.

Chapter 10

"Nice to you see you're back," I said to Sonya who sat behind her desk again. "Two more nights until weekend." Her eyes were a little swollen and her nose was red. She looked at me with a dull stare. Even sick Sonya wasn't much of a party. If anything it annoyed her more when I didn't act like I wanted to kill her.

"No papers tonight?" I asked when she didn't hand me a stack of papers like she usually did.

"No, tonight you get to be humane," she said in an icy voice. It was nice to know she had some emotions, albeit negative ones. I'd long ago gotten over being upset when people didn't think I was lovable. You had to be able to do cute and cuddly for that. I didn't do cute and cuddly.

I walked through to Ruben's office and opened the closed door without knocking.

"You're late," he said.

"I'm here," I countered. "And you don't have work for me anyway, it seems. I don't know what you're upset about."

Ruben leaned back in his chair and stretched up his arms. His shirt had ketchup stains down the front.

"You're not prioritizing my clients like I asked," he said. I rolled my eyes and sat down on the chair opposite him.

"Don't get comfortable, you're hitting the streets in less than a minute."

"What am I supposed to do if I can't find him?" I asked.

"You're going to make sure you do. I'm not giving you any other cases tonight so you get to take all the time you need to locate your mark. Don't say I don't ever do anything for you."

"I can't go to my contact," I said. Ruben looked up at me. This was my cue to explain.

"He's having... technical trouble." It was close enough to the truth. Having your monitors kicked in was pretty technical.

"Well, you're resourceful. I'm sure you'll find a way."

I got up and turned for the door without saying anything.

"I want this guy before the weekend, Adele," Ruben said and there was a warning in his voice.

"I can't do more than I can do, Ruben. You know better than to make me promise."

"I'm not making you promise. *I'm* promising. This one has consequences."

I walked out because it sounded too much like a threat. I didn't respond well to threats – I tended to turn on them and be the one that was threatening. And when I threatened, I didn't let it hang. I finished the job.

When I stood outside I looked up and down the road. It was empty, the halogen lamps casting circles of light into the otherwise dark street. Very few people were around. It was common sense not to be out on the street in Westham's downtown at night. I tried to decide where I was going to go.

I couldn't go to Joel, for obvious reason. Aspen was out of the question because I was supposed to be on duty and she didn't have a nocturnal cycle like me. And the sad fact was that that was the total sum of people I knew. Besides my dad, who I'd already seen and hoped not to see again if I could help it, and Connor who I was seeing way too much of for a mark.

I sighed.

My life was complicated as hell, even when nothing was happening in it.

The only thing left was to try and trace the person that had attacked me. She'd had a reason. Maybe it was something we could talk out. And by talking out I meant with the business end of my gun staring her in the face. But how was I going to do that?

All I knew about her was that she couldn't be human, and she had it in for me. It wasn't a hell of a lead to go by.

I got on my bike and drove up to Westham Hill. I'd seen her there last. I doubted she'd been following me, or else I would have seen her in other places. Unless she'd meant to stay away, which was just as possible. My idea was that I'd run into her by accident. She knew who I was and what I did, but she hadn't meant to go after me. If that was the case she'd had to be monitoring the house in Caldwell Street, the same way I had. Or something.

So if that was what it had been, that was where I was going to start. What did I have to lose? Only my life. No biggy.

I scolded myself. I might have been running after a dead end.

A person suddenly popped up in the beam of light my bike cast on the road, and I pulled both brakes and stepped down hard with my foot. My bike squealed and turned to the side, skidding forward. I gasped, hearing my own panic fill my helmet.

I slid on the tarmac, the rough road tearing and ripping into my leather pants. The sickening sound of the road ripping up my paint filled the night.

When I finally came to a stop I jumped up and looked around me. Where had the person gone? I inspected myself. My leather pants were torn all the way down the outside of my left leg. Dammit. Leathers weren't cheap. At least it was better than being ripped raw myself. I was grazed a little, I could feel the fresh wound running down my leg, but it wouldn't be deep. Only skin, no flesh. This was partly why I wore leathers – they were thick enough to protect me from a scrape. I picked up my bike and tried to start it. With luck it hadn't flooded, but the paint job was horribly scratched. It hurt me more than my leg would tomorrow. My bike was one of the few things I got sentimental about. I usually distanced myself emotionally to spare myself. But a bike I could trust.

I was becoming delusional. There was no one around me.

All of this is going to catch up with you a voice swirled around me like a warm breeze. It was everywhere around me, and in my head, all at once. I was pretty sure it was hers. *I'm watching you. You can run, princess, but you can't hide.*

It was sickening and I had my knife out, even though there was nothing I could stab. A cackling laughter enveloped me and it made me feel useless and naïve.

I was furious. Humiliated that I'd fallen, angry that my paintjob was messed up, horrified that I could be haunted by someone that was still alive.

"Come out and face me, coward!" I shouted into the night. My voice broke around the edges of my sentence like cracked glass. She had to be here somewhere to mess with my mind like that. Supernatural creatures had all sorts of powers, but they also had ranges. She couldn't find me if I was too far away, unless she had my blood. And I knew for a fact she didn't. I had enough vampire in me to know my blood and what it felt like when someone else had some of it.

The laughing sound danced around me again, mocking me, and then it faded like a lost echo. The final throes of her laughter melted away.

Suddenly she was in front of me. Her hair was ice-white in the moonlight and this time her face wasn't hidden in the shadows. She had a sharp, cat-like face and her eyes glowed green in the dark. Not pools of black like before. I would bet everything I had that she had some sort of feline characteristics and powers. She stood a couple of feet away from me. She wore a leather outfit that was a lot sexier than mine, I had to admit. I wondered if I should do something about my own clothes, but then I told myself I was a killer not a temptress.

A smile lit up her eyes even more, and I realized she was still toying with my mind. Jealousy, self-doubt, materialistic values. I'd heard of something like her before but I couldn't quite grasp it. There were creatures out there that could mess with your mind, bring up all sorts of thoughts and emotions, enough to destroy you without them even doing anything at all.

"You take a while to catch on," she said in a syrupy voice that I didn't trust at all.

"I don't have all night." Actually, I did. But I wasn't going to let her last that long.

She was quicker than I thought. With a blast of cold air she was right in front of me, our faces so close they almost touched. A sharp pain shot into my cheek. Her nails were colored red by my blood. The bitch had scratched me and she'd done it so fast I hadn't seen it coming.

I touched my cheek gingerly and my fingers came away slick with blood. I swore. I was starting to wonder if I wasn't outmatched.

"You swear like a man," she said.

"You fight like a girl." So it wasn't my most creative come back, but I had to say something before I launched at her because she was putting me on my ass so fast I couldn't keep up. I had to win this one. I wasn't the type that was accustomed to losing.

She let out a feline scream when I jumped on her and we tumbled to the ground in a tangle of limbs. I tried to grab a handful of hair but it was platted down in a complicated twirl that didn't give me much of a grip.

"You need to up your beauty skills," she said and she drew my mind to my own hair. It was in a ponytail, the black hair streaming down my back. As she redirected my mind she grabbed a handful and yanked. Her hand came away with strands of hair streaming in between her fingers.

I balled my fist and hit her square in the mouth. Who said I was scared to hit a girl? It bloomed red the moment my hand left her face and she spat on the ground in a very feminine way. I was being slapped around like a child, and I had to make my mark quick if I wanted this fight to carry on equally.

"You're going to regret doing that," she said, her voice still charming as ever. I reached for my knife. The silver had done the trick last time. I held it up, poised the blade to sink it into her chest. But her green eyes suddenly caught mine, and her pupils expanded until there was nothing left of her irises. Only black holes that fell into a void of nothing. It was welcoming, beckoning me into a world of oblivion. Of bliss. I could leave all this behind and escape to a place where my life didn't exist. Where I didn't exist.

No, I had to fight it. My thoughts were almost like a fading echo in my own mind, but I focused on them. I couldn't let her steal me away from myself. I blinked my eyes and tried to look away, but something held my gaze. Something powerful. Something invisible.

"It's a pity I'm not allowed to kill you," she whispered, her voice rolling around my mind in waves. "It would have been so much fun to watch you bleed out. But my masters have a bone to pick with you. So I only get to play."

She ran a finger down my other cheek and it left a trail of fire behind. I wanted to fight back, but my body was numb and I couldn't move my limbs. All I could feel was the emptiness, beckoning to me. All I could see were those bottomless pits and the whites of her eyes glowing fluorescent green.

Chapter 11

I blinked my eyes. They were foggy and I kept blinking to clear my vision. Slowly the room around me came into focus, and I found myself staring at my own ceiling.

I sat up. Soft morning light filtered into the bedroom. I grabbed my phone where it lay face down on the nightstand, and checked it. It was eight-thirty, Friday morning. I hadn't lost too much time. A million questions crashed down on me.

How had I gotten home? What had happened after the fight last night? I groaned, the weight of humiliation dragging me down like a weight around my ankles; if a fight was even what I could call it. Where had the rest of the night gone? What had I done in the black void that stretched from then until now?

I couldn't remember anything. The last thing I remembered were those eyes, black pools of emptiness that drew me. The warmth came back, the numb feeling that I had been craving for years. The feeling I had never been able to find with any of my kills.

I sat up and shook my head. I had to snap out of it. She was going to steal everything from me. Everything that made me, me. I knew it, like a solid truth inside me, cementing my resolve in place.

When I threw back the cover and swung my legs out, I noticed I was still wearing my leathers. The graze on my leg smarted and I touched my thigh gingerly. Hadn't I gotten undressed? I felt like I'd been stuck in a dream. I got up, unbuckled my thigh sheath and climbed out of the torn pants. The leather clung to my wounds, and peeling them off was like removing a Band-Aid. I threw them toward the bin. I stripped of the rest of my clothes as well.

I slathered antiseptic cream on the wound that burned an angry red all the way down the length of my leg. It hurt like hell and I could feel my pulse throbbing down the length of my leg. The last thing I wanted was an infection the size of half my body. At least being half-vampire meant I would heal up in half the time. When I'd finished I took an inventory of my stuff.

All my guns were in the gun safe. Normal. But my thigh sheath had still been on my leg. Strange. I walked over to the bed. My Glock was missing. When I searched through the room I found it on the dressing table. Wrong.

In the bathroom I checked myself out in the mirror. I ran my hands down my face, and opened the tap. I cupped my hands under the stream and I was just about to splash cold water onto my face. I looked at myself in the mirror again. My old bruises were completely gone. She'd scratched me hard on the cheek, I remembered how it had stung, the slick blood running down my face. I inspected my skin. There wasn't a mark. I tried to count how many hours it had been. Seven? Eight? I could heal up in that time with half my vampire healing abilities. But it felt quicker than normal. Either I was showing more vampire side, which scared me, or something else was wrong – I'd missed more time or something. It scared me too, so I decided to believe the former.

Still, it all felt wrong. Very wrong.

I still felt the humiliation of the scratch, the fact that I hadn't seen it coming, they'd I'd gotten beaten up by a girl. Again.

I fetched my knife in its sheath from the bedroom and hung it in the shower. I wasn't going to do this one without protection. I wasn't going to do anything without protection anymore, until I could figure out what the hell was going on. The hot water stung down my leg and I gritted my teeth, trying to keep soap out of the wound.

By the time I was finished showering two things played in my mind. One: She was just toying with me now, like a cat playing with a mouse. But the real trouble would come. She wouldn't let me live. If I was getting beaten up already, how would I protect myself when things got serious?

And two: if I had gotten home by myself that would have been fine, but there were too many things that pointed to someone else trying to fake my routine. That meant that someone knew me well enough to know what I did and where I lived. And if that was the case, I was in very, very deep trouble.

The phone rang and I nearly jumped out of my skin. I picked it up. I didn't recognize the number.

"Hello?" My voice was thin, unsure. I hated the way I sounded.

"It's Jennifer," the feminine voice sounded in my ear, and I could feel every fiber in my body slowly relax. I breathed out, a release. My entire body was tight, my muscles strung out. I rubbed my temple with my free hand.

"I was just wondering if you've managed to find anything yet," Jennifer said.

Yes, I found your boyfriend. He was a vampire and I really wanted to see him again.

"Actually, I was hoping we could meet in person again. There are a couple of things I'd like to talk about."

"We can talk now," she suggested.

"I don't think this is the kind of thing we want to talk about on the phone."

She gasped on the other end of the line and dropped her voice. "Do you think it's being tapped?"

This wasn't a spy novel. Things weren't like that. Blood, betrayal, death, that was a part of my daily life. But tapping phones didn't seem likely. I thought back to Joel, his pit being trashed. The level of security on Connor's online information. I shook it off.

"Nothing like that. I just want to meet up. When will suit you?"

"Saturday afternoon," she said after thinking a moment. "We can meet at my home."

I hesitated for a second, but then agreed. If it wasn't my home it would be hers. I hated being out in public, and I wasn't willing to let her into my home again unless I didn't have a choice.

"I'll be there at three," I answered. "Send me your address."

"Will you let me know if you find anything in the meantime?"

"I will," I lied. I was a terrible person.

"Truth is I'm starting to lose hope," she said and a pang of guilt shot through my chest. What was I doing? I was working myself into a corner, and fast. In the beginning of the week my life was regular. Shoot to kill, survive to see another night, take care of Aspen. Simple. Now I didn't even know which side was up anymore. My life had become a Rubik Cube I couldn't solve.

When Jennifer hung up I dialed the office. Boy was Ruben going to be pissed. Not only did I manage to fail his orders and find Connor, but I had also lost an entire night.

"What?" he barked into the phone when he picked up.

"I wanted to explain last night," I answered. This wasn't going to be easy. I expected him to swear up the one side of me and down the other.

"What about last night?" he asked. "You have more information you want to share with me?"

"More?"

"Than last night."

I hesitated. "Did I phone in last night?"

Ruben snorted. "You told me you'd found a lead and you were tracing him. Not your best effort but it's better than nothing. What's going on?"

Someone was playing with me. Nothing made sense, and most of all, Ruben wasn't angry with me. Something was definitely off.

"I just phoned to check what time you needed me in tonight," I recovered. I didn't want him to find out something was wrong. I needed this job more than I needed the money.

"Don't come in tonight. Something urgent came up and I'm not going to be in the office. I gave Carl a night off too." I'd completely forgotten about my so-called colleague. It usually felt like I was working the field alone. I hardly ran into the guy. Why hadn't Ruben assigned him to Connor's case if he thought I was making such a mess of it? Also, having a night off was a rarity.

"I'll be in touch," Ruben said before I could ask and hung up the phone. A night off. I couldn't remember when last that had happened. It sounded good for a moment. Until I started wondering what I would do with my time. What I would do for a release instead.

I put more antiseptic cream on my wound, and then bandaged me leg up. It restricted my movement, which I hated, but with some luck it would be healed soon. I got dressed into jeans and a blouse. I let my hair loose for a change and left the apartment.

I had a couple of errands to run. I'd run out of leather clothes and I wasn't going to do the dirty in jeans. It just wasn't that easy to get blood out of regular material. I also needed a quote on my paint job, I had to train with Sensei and I needed to get to a place where I could do research about the cat lady whose name I still didn't know. I was running out of adjectives.

I was getting tired of referring to her as my attacker. I would have much preferred to refer to her as my victim, but for that I'd need a leg up on what she was capable of.

The rest of Friday was ridiculous. I went home with my bike booked in for a paint job, new leathers in plastic bags and absolutely nothing anywhere on women who had the abilities of Miss Mittens. I was miserable and tired, so instead of heading out, I took two sleeping pills and crawled under the pillows. As if my internal clock wasn't messed up enough as it was.

Saturday morning my cellphone pulled me out of a comatose kind of sleep with a shrill ring that made me want to throw it through the window. Instead I answered. No one said I had a lack of self-control.

"What is it?"

"This is Sonya," her dull voice came over the phone. I realized she'd never phoned me before. I was usually in the office at sundown. If anything she sounded more boring than in person. I wondered if she had a life outside the office.

"You work on weekends? You're phoning me in the day." I imagined her in a room with metal shutters and black curtains.

She ignored my question. "Ruben has a meeting set up you need to attend," she said.

"You may work weekends, but I don't."

"You had the night off," she pointed out. Of course. Why would I think I'd get paid leave? "He wants you to meet with Miss Clemens today at noon."

"Miss Clemens the reporter?" The name at the bottom of the article Joel had shown me.

"That's the one."

"It's daytime," I said. Ruben and I had agreed, even though we both knew that I could head out in the day. I just didn't want to.

You'll make a plan. Meet Ruben at Fiasco just before noon."

She hung up. I sighed and let the phone slide down onto the pillow. Great. If I knew I would trade my weekend for a Friday night off I would have refused and gone out anyway. I didn't even know how I was going to get a hold of Connor to cancel with him. He would just have to suck it. Work came before vampires. This was besides that work *was* vampires.

I rolled out of bed and crawled into the shower, swearing when the hot water stung enough to remind me of my leg. The edges were healed with new pink skin, but the graze was still quite big and it hurt. The hot water woke my body up slowly, and

by the time I was finished I felt human again. I texted Aspen. I
didn't like skipping days, but I would see her tomorrow.

I stood in front of my closet with a towel wrapped around my
body, looking for something appropriate to wear. I wasn't going
to meet the snooping reporter in my killing clothes. There was
nothing that screamed trouble like a woman like me with guns
and leathers. I settled on jeans that could stretch to allow for the
bandage I wrapped around my leg, a wine red blouse that made
my hair color intense, and black sandals. The shoes were still in
the original shoe box Aspen had given them to me in, three
birthdays ago.

I applied make-up and brushed my hair. I even went through
the effort of putting on earrings. When I studied the final result
in the mirror I didn't look like myself at all. I looked like a
business woman. A civilian. Someone who could have a
completely different life. Pity that changing what I looked like
didn't change who I was.

Fiasco was a coffee shop in the center across from the mall. It
was the place everyone went to for business meetings because it
opened at six in the morning before rush hour, and it offered the
paper with a coffee and bagel as its morning special. When I
arrived Ruben was already at a table. He wore suite pants and a
collared shirt with a tie. The shirt was ironed and clean and he'd
run a comb through his hair. I glanced down to see shiny black
shoes instead of slippers.

"You clean up nicely. You look human for a change," Ruben
said when I sat down.

"I can say the same for you," I responded coolly. He snorted.

"I was scared you might arrive in your leathers."

"What kind of an accountant would I be if I wore leathers?"

"That's my girl," Ruben said, smiling. I wanted to tell him
how much I wasn't his girl, but before I could another woman
arrived at our table. She introduced herself and Celia Clemens,
journalist for the Westham Gazette. I didn't know why she

bothered with the title. There was only one newspaper in town. The Gazette had a monopoly that claimed all the stories right off the bat. No competitors? Tough life.

I looked at her carefully. She had mouse-brown hair pulled back in a low bun, and glasses with rims that stretched across half of her face. She had sharp features, almost pixie-like but something tugged at the back of mine. Something familiar. She wore an off-green dress suit that did nothing for her skin tone, and her eyes were a dark brown. Her clothes dated from a time-period that suggested she was rolling on to her forties, but her smooth skin and lack of smile-wrinkles told me otherwise. She couldn't have been much older than thirty. I would bank on late twenties if the glossy quality of her skin was anything to go by. Not the gloss of riches, but the gloss of those who would live longer than others.

"I appreciate you making the time to meet with me," she said to Ruben in a sweet voice. Her words were lilted at the edges, but again there was something familiar about it. Almost like there was a veil between me and her, and if I could just remove it I would know I'd seen her before.

"Of course, Miss Clemens," Ruben answered, equally charming.

"Celia, please," she said and took a small notepad out of her briefcase.

"I just have a couple of questions for you," she said. She never made eye contact with me. I didn't know if I should feel insulted or flattered.

"Go on," Ruben said, and Celia started her questioning. It was the standard stuff. What kind of business Ruben ran, how long he'd been doing it, how many employees, that sort of thing. I had no idea why she was bothering at all.

"Word has it you operate at night, as well," Celia said, and Ruben's face closed.

"We have a team that works overtime often," he said. His voice was guarded. "It's common knowledge that we employ vampires."

"You are pro-vampire then, I assume?"

Ruben was everything but pro-vampire.

"I do what is necessary to keep my company in the right circles. There are laws about everything these days, and who am I to keep someone out of business just because they're..." he looked at me when he said the last word. "Different."

I could feel the tension in the air building like an electric storm. Ruben's face was expressionless but I could smell his panic. Celia wasn't throwing off any kind of emotion at all, and that had me on alert. People always threw off some kind of scent or emotions. Excitement, fear, sadness. Even something as simple as interest had a smell and a feel to it. Celia should have had at least that. And she didn't.

"There are rumors doing the rounds that you're the person to come to when someone has a problem." Trouble.

"We've always helped people with their finances, our main goal is to help our clients make ends meet." It was a relatively smooth if he didn't look so panicked.

"Now, Mr. Cross. We both know that wasn't what I was talking about."

"Do we?" he answered. Good for Ruben. He was starting to play this game the right way.

"What do you do?" she suddenly turned to me, and her eyes sent a shock through my body that I couldn't place but it wasn't altogether unfamiliar. It made my fingertips tingle and my legs felt warm. This was not natural for a human.

"I'm an accountant with Cross Ledger," I answered without missing a beat. Ruben might have been panicking but I was ready for her. Miss Clemens was trying to hide who she really was. I did it all the time, I recognized the signs. The only question now was, who was she really?

Celia had a glint in her eye. She sat back in her chair, like she didn't have a care in the world, her one leg crossed over the other. Her skirt rode up a little, and on the skin just above her knee was a burn mark. A couple of days old, a scar now, it was red and flaring anymore.

It caught my attention, and I knew right away that burn was out of place. Household accidents didn't leave a scar like that. It was about three inches long and slightly off-kilter.

"Miss Clemens," I said, interrupting her questioning. Ruben looked relieved. She looked at me, annoyed. She wanted to be the one in control of this conversation. Too bad. When I looked into her eyes, I noticed the black was complete. The realization knocked me off-balance and I fought to maintain composure.

"That looks like a painful burn mark on your leg," I said. She looked down at her leg and tugged the skirt down to hide it.

"Cooking accident," she said. "I'm clumsy in the kitchen." Sure. Straight burn marks, the length of a blade. What was she doing, kitchen gymnastics?

Her eyes settled on mine again, and her words suddenly seemed too believable. *Kitchen accidents happen all the time. I didn't cook often, but burns are common in the kitchen. Stop it* my mind shouted at her and I forced her out of it. I'd nailed her. There was only one person I'd run into that could play mind games like that.

"I'll bet you are," I said. My voice was calm, but the atmosphere changed. It became thick, laced with warning and threat. I suddenly smelled her emotions. A powerful stench like flowers, the perfume-like smell that came after they'd been parched. I'd smelled that scent before. It was also laced with danger. No anger or fear, just trouble.

"Where was I?" she asked Ruben but she was still looking at me.

"You were talking about hidden identities and double lives," I said without missing a beat. It wasn't what she'd been talking about at all. I was calling her out. Ruben looked from me to Celia and back. He was starting to realize he'd missed something.

I couldn't be sure this was her. After all, this one had brown hair and the other had had white hair. But I had started running into creatures that could disguise themselves, and the only time I would believe what I was seeing, was never.

"I think that's enough for today," she said. Her voice was confident. I didn't think she fled because she was exposed. Her reaction wasn't panicked. She was leaving because she'd found what she was looking for. Me.

"Thank you for coming," Ruben started saying, but Celia stood up and walked away just as the waitress arrive.

"Can I take your order?" she asked with a bright smile. Ruben shook his head and waved her away.

"What was that all about?"

"Hundred bucks says Celia Clemens is only an alias," I said as we both watched her walk away. "Not the name, but the job, definitely." An alias or she had a damn good cover. Better than mine if she could throw her name around in public. "You'd better get some sort of insurance, Ruben. I have a feeling you're not going to last very long."

"I'll get right on it," he said. He was taking my word for it. It was a first. Maybe he'd realized somewhere along the lines that he was in over his head, and I knew more about this ugly world than he did.

"I need to go," I said to Ruben.

"I want you in the office at midnight," Ruben said when I turned to leave.

"Why?" Midnight was the witching hour. That was when supernatural creatures were most alive, the time I either wanted to be out with my guns, or locked up safely at home.

"My clients want answers about why the job isn't done yet, and I'm not going to make excuses for you again. I'm not facing them alone, you can come in and deal with them with me."

"In the middle of the night?"

"It's the only time slot they have available."

I opened my mouth to argue, but instead I closed it again and nodded. I would be there, why not? I needed a bit of action, and maybe if I knew why they wanted Connor dead it would give me enough motivation to push my pathetic attraction aside and finish the job.

"I'll be there," I said.

A midnight meeting over the weekend sounded like a lot of fun. Not. I was sure I would run into some creatures that didn't show their faces in the day, and I wasn't sure I wanted to. But if Ruben was involved I had to. He was just a human, and even though I strongly disliked him, this job was my responsibility. His increasing anxiety over the kill had me on my guard, too. Ruben didn't just get upset when I didn't make a kill right away.

First, though, I had to get to Jennifer. She'd texted me her address and I had half an hour to get to her. I felt stranded without my bike, but this was the way it had to be. I blamed Celia. No doubt about it.

I took the bus and it dropped me off halfway up Westham Hills. She lived in Tambuca Crescent, one up from Caldwell. I was starting to get to know this area. When I walked to number twenty one, I pushed the button on the intercom and a woman with an accent answered.

"Adele Griffin for Jennifer Lawson, please," I said. The intercom clicked and the massive gates swung open, revealing a curling driveway that led up to a Tuscan style house with arches over balconies and hanging plants.

The door opened and a woman with a maid's outfit from the movies and dark skin answered the door. I'd half-expected a butler.

"Please follow me," she said and took me to a formal sitting room just off the entrance hall. It was mostly white, with splashes of mahogany and red here and there. "Miss Lawson will be with you now."

When Jennifer arrived she wore a flowing green dress the color of her eyes, and she glided to the armchair opposite me. Her hair was impossibly straight and her make-up was flawless. If this was how she dressed on a Saturday I wondered how she dressed for an event.

"Thank you for taking the time to meet with me," she said and the maid brought in a tray with a tea pot and cups that sat upside down on their saucers. They were accompanied by a glass bowl filled with sugar cookies. "You look nice."

"Business meeting," I said and wished I didn't look like a mannequin in a window display. Jennifer turned the cups around and poured tea. I took a cookie and nibbled on it. I felt out of place here, surrounded by everything that never mattered.

"You lied to me," I said, getting right down to business. Jennifer's hands trembled slightly, but other than that she was composed and her voice was steady when she answered me.

"What do you mean?"

"You didn't tell me about the trafficking. The fact that Connor was wanted."

She looked up at me and her green eyes were bright like emeralds.

"You found out."

"Did you think this was something you could keep a secret from me?" I asked. It seemed a little stupid for someone this high up to make an assumption like that.

"I suppose you would... I just thought, when I first found out you didn't know, that I could ask you to do this for me and you wouldn't be influence by what they were saying about him."

"And about you," I said. Because that was what it was really about.

She didn't answer. Instead her lips were pursed and slightly pouted, and she paid particular attention to the second cup of tea she poured, which she offered to me. I took it to be polite. I hated tea.

"You are going to have to be honest with me. You came to me because of Connor, saying you needed me to find him. But you knew he wasn't human anymore, didn't you?"

She looked at me and guessed that I would know if she was lying. She couldn't know that I could smell a lie, but it was a smart move.

"I've been to hell and back since I took this job, and I'm not going to get beaten up for nothing," I said.

"She found you, then?" Jennifer asked, and I didn't have to ask to know she was talking about the cat lady. Celia.

"Are you involved with this?" I asked. Direct was usually the best way to go. When you embroidered a picture around facts, danced around the truth, the chances were that the person you were talking to would do the same. A straight forward question was difficult to avoid without making it obvious.

"I'm not," she said. "I don't condone things like that."

"But you don't condone vampirism either," I said. This was a guess, but it was an accurate one. Her face turned to stone and when she looked at me a lot of the color in her eyes had drained. "Why did you come to me?"

"I hoped that if you found Connor before they did—"

"You knew what it would mean for me to get into this, and you still sent me in there without the facts. That's like going into battle unarmed, Jennifer. Do you have any idea what it's like?"

She took a sip, looking at me with big green eyes over the edge of the cup. She shuddered.

"I needed him to stay alive. I needed them not to be able to find him. I can't love a vampire, Adele. Surely you of all people can understand?"

A million different emotions ran through me. I could understand. I killed them. My mother loved one and look where that ended up. I met Connor. And then everything about him, even in his vampire state, drew me to him. He was irresistible. I could love that vampire.

"Did you know about the trafficking?" I asked. She nodded slowly. "Even before Connor did?"

"They asked me help them, to keep it a secret so he wouldn't find out. They needed his funds."

"And you agreed?"

She sighed. "I don't know how to make this sound like it's not wrong. I was only looking out for his best interests. We were going to get married. I couldn't let a scandal like that ruin it."

"Because you love him so much?"

When she looked up at me again her eyes were filled with tears. I fought the urge to roll my eyes. I was being the epitome of politeness.

"Can't you understand that?" she asked.

"Actually I can't, no," I said. Honesty was your best policy. I couldn't imagine loving someone enough that something like trafficking couldn't ruin it. I often argued I didn't have morals. Maybe I was wrong. "Besides, I think you did it for the money."

"They weren't paying me for my silence!" she said, her cheeks ashen.

I shook my head. I was going out on a limb here. Her reactions guided me. "I'm not talking about their money. I'm talking about his."

She gasped and the air around us became cold. Not the supernatural kind of cold, but the kind that came with a person realizing she'd talked herself into a corner and there was no way to get out of it again.

"I can't lose it all. I won't go back to the hole I was in when my ex-husband left me."

Ex? This whole thing had suddenly turned to a saga I didn't want to be closely involved in.

"Look, I don't want to hear from you again. You lied to me, and you got me in a mess where if I don't do something soon, I have a feeling people are going to die. You better hope to god that doesn't include me, because you signed off on my death sentence by not letting me know what this was about."

The tears that had sat on the rims of her eyelids spilled over her cheeks now.

"I knew it," she whispered. "I'm doomed either way, then."

Yeah, sure. Don't' worry about your fiancé or his health, his life. Or mine. Just about your own. I knew better than to speak any of those words out loud, but people like Jennifer disgusted me.

"I have to go," I said. I'd had just about enough of this house, the riches, the urge for something that didn't matter at all. The betrayal.

She stood up without a word and walked me to the door. I walked down the driveway, curling around the trees along with it, and when I stood outside the gate and it closed firmly shut behind me, I let out a breath I didn't know I'd been holding.

This was the last time I was going to try help someone.

Chapter 12

I got a call from the workshop telling me my bike was ready. I stopped by and picked it up. I wasn't going to spend more time without my bike, come what may.

I looked up at the sky. The sun was low, touching the horizon. It was time I met Connor. Unease swirled in my stomach like nausea. What was I doing? I couldn't keep doing this. I had to go there and kill him, get it over with. That was what I would do.

I drove to Mulberry Street and sat in the road, finger stroking the stake absently while I turned it all over in my head. I was going to march in there and push the stake into his heart, break my promise because that was what I did. I broke things. Or maybe I was going to use my Smith & Wesson and blow his head off. I was going to do this.

I closed my eyes and breathed, ready to walk up to him and finished the job... when I sent my feelers out, and the house was empty. Connor wasn't home.

Disappointment lodged in my chest and dragged me down like it was made of lead. I wouldn't get to see him, then. I wasn't sure why I was upset. Was it because I couldn't see him, or because I wouldn't get the chance to kill him? We had an appointment. Wasn't I important enough?

I started the bike and flew down the street, embracing the roar of the engine that surrounded me and the hum of the speed in my blood. Not tonight. I wouldn't have to kill him tonight. But at some point, I'd have to.

I swallowed hard. This was the most difficult job to date, and killing people was particularly easy, as a rule.

The office was cold and dark when I arrived just before midnight. I parked a block away so my bike's engine wouldn't announce my arrival. I wasn't a girl that liked an entrance. I wore my leathers and I felt comfortable and at home in my body again. I climbed the stairs, trying to ignore the pain every time I bent my leg. I got to the second floor and walked through Sonya's deserted office and into Ruben's. Apparently she did take a break now and then. A dim lamp on his desk was the only source of light in the room. Ruben sat at his desk looking worn and haggard, like a lifetime had passed between now and the afternoon's meeting. A faint smell of alcohol hung in the air.

"Don't you just look like a ray of sunshine," I said to him. He looked up at me like he wasn't fully registering my presence.

"What's wrong?" I asked. My back was up immediately, and I opened my senses. I'd been careless. The office had never been a danger zone. But now warning in a thin trace of terror hung in the air. Ruben's terror, if something didn't subdue him as much as it did. The alcohol smell was also a rouse. Something that intended to throw me off.

A dark shadow stepped out of a corner, and I jumped. The feeling intensified. The man was tall, wearing a black duster like cowboys in the movies. His skin and hair was pale, and he wore black wrap-around glasses, and he wasn't a man at all. This was a vampire. No wonder Ruben looked like death warmed up. He didn't usually come face to face with the underworld, not like this. He only employed them, but we took contracts from humans.

Another shadow appeared almost behind me. The only reason I knew it was there was because I smelled it before it had moved. I couldn't see it but I felt it coming closer.

"Stop right there," I said with a low voice filled with warning. The first vampire chuckled when I spoke.

"So this is your assassin? A woman? No wonder she hasn't been able to get the job done."

"I wouldn't be so quick with the insults if I were you," I said. Ruben didn't respond. The thigh sheath and the two guns on my side and at my back burned imprints against my skin. My fingers itched to use them, but I wasn't going to jump the gun. With two large vampires, me and a defenseless human in a small office it was better not to jump right into fighting if it wasn't necessary. Blood shed needed space and a lack of human audience.

"You want O'Neill dead," I said matter-of-factly. The vampire nodded. I was aware of his partner moving around the office, probably listening and feeling for the presence of people or other vampires.

"You're not doing what we asked," the vampire said. "We're becoming impatient."

"Why do you need me to do it?" I asked. "You look like you have what it takes to do it yourself."

The vampire laughed a low evil laugh that danced across my skin and I broke out in shivers. I hated them off the bat, but this was worse. This vampire was powerful, more so than the ones I'd been hunting for so long. More powerful than my father had ever been. Where did the vampires that felt like this hang out? I realized I'd been dealing with the bottom of the food chain.

"Let's just say it's in our best interest not to be tied to the murder."

"She's on the case, I told you," Ruben spoke for the first time. His voice was dull and without inflection or emotion.

The vampire ignored him.

"He wasn't supposed to live through the change in the first place, but he did. Now you need to get rid of him."

So they were the ones that had dumped him in the alley.

"He's getting away from you, isn't he?" I asked. My tone was mocking and I smiled although none of this was friendly. "You can't find him, and it's ticking you off that you have to ask for help."

The vampire in front of me scowled and the air turned ice cold around us. Frost formed on the window, on the inside, and crawled up the lamp stand. I shivered. Vampires this strong could only be masters. They were old, very old, and they had far more control than the everyday newbies I dealt with.

"You should know better than to mock me," the vampire said in a hiss, his voice spitting and I could almost feel it on my skin.

"It looks like she needs some motivation," the other vampire said in a gravelly voice that sent a bolt of fear into my body. His eyes slid to Ruben. I readied myself to grab my gun the moment something happened. But they hadn't meant a fight. Instead the first vampire laughed again, like I was a child that tried to play grown-up games.

"You've met Celia," the vampire said, and the icy finger traced the outlines of my body when he mentioned her name. I nodded slowly. He wasn't talking about the reporter she'd come disguised as. He was referring to the woman that had been playing games with me. The cat.

"I can't say it was a pleasure. She needs to be put on a leash."

"She's perfectly in control. She only does what we tell her to. She more like... a pet."

"A pet that needs to be put down," I spat. I glanced at Ruben. He was hanging on his desk his eyes staring into nothing. I could smell his fear, but his face was calm. They had him under some sort of spell that kept him drug-like. If he were left to his own devices he would probably have panicked or tried to escape. Or worse. People turned crazy when fear took over.

The other vampire, the one that wasn't the obvious leader, pointed a gun at Ruben. So they had guns too. They were faster than me. I wondered if I jumped at them, if I would be faster than a bullet to get to Ruben.

"You have a lot of anger in you," the leader said. He could smell my emotions better than I could smell his. He waved at his friend and the vampire lowered the gun. I felt like I could breathe again. Threatening Ruben's life was foul play. "I don't know if that will be enough."

"Enough for what?" I asked. My voice was hard and I imagined taking my S&W and blowing his head right off.

"Enough to save her."

Fear rippled through my body and suddenly every thought of violence was gone, replaced by my sister's face. The smell of fear permeated the room, sour and vile, and the vampires both laughed.

"Yes, that's the one. Your sister, I believe. You've worked hard to cover her up, but we found out anyway."

"Don't you dare!" I shouted. All control was gone now. Yep, crazy with fear.

I pulled out my gun and pointed it at the vampire in front of me. They were both strong enough to overthrow me. They could have beaten me to a pulp right there and no training in the world would have prepared me. They could have killed me in an instant. But neither of them moved. The vampire I pointed my gun at was surprisingly calm looking down the barrel of a gun that could finish it, but that was because he knew as well as I that it wasn't going save Aspen. And if it wasn't, I wouldn't do it.

"Finish the job, and we'll leave you alone," the second vampire said. "It's not difficult. A life for a life. Take Connor's we'll spare hers, or you can have it the other way round. You let us know which you prefer."

They both dematerialized with a whoosh that pushed Ruben's papers off his desk. The small office, filled with their presence until now, was suddenly cold and empty. Ruben's eyes lost their glazed quality and he looked up at me.

"God I hate it when they do that to me."

"I gather it wasn't the first time," I said. Ruben shook his head.

"I told you they were dangerous. Just finish the job, Adele. Dammit." He pushed himself upright in his chair and rubbed his eyes. Then he dragged his hands down over his cheeks, deforming his face for a second.

I looked at Ruben, and suddenly I couldn't breathe. It was like I'd turned to lead. I doubled over, clamping my arms over my stomach, trying to stop the terrible pain that sliced through me. My head spun and I felt like I was going to throw up.

"They're going to kill her," I said, dry heaving. There were no tears. Only the fear making my blood thick in my veins and forcing my body into the kind of submission I'd only felt once before, when she'd nearly died the first time.

"Come on, Adele," Ruben said, tugging at my arm, trying to pull me back to reality. "Keep it together." He sounded panicked. That made two of us. "Just kill him, and then it will all be over."

He was right. The panic left my body as quickly as it had come, and I unfolded myself, peeling myself off the floor. I took a deep breath and closed my eyes, finding all my pieces and forcing them back together.

"I need to go," I said, sounding controlled again.

"You know, this is the first time I've ever seen you lose it," he said.

"We all have our demons, Ruben. I'm sure you have things in your life that reduce you to a pile of fear."

Ruben nodded. "After this, vampires," he said.

I walked into the night, the air filling my lungs like I hadn't breathed before. The open sky above me was freedom after the jail the little office had become. I looked at the time. It was one, but I took a chance and dialed anyway. Aspen's sleepy voice sounded just before the phone would roll over to voicemail.

"Are you okay?" I asked.

"I'm fine," she said and yawned. Relief flooded my body and I felt like my knees would buckle under my weight. "What's going on?"

"Nothing, angel. Go back to bed."

"You've only ever called me that when something was really wrong."

"I'm taking care of it," I said and hung up. Because I was. I was going to save my sister. There wasn't a question in my mind about who I would choose when it came down to it. Aspen would win out every single time, no matter how much Connor amused me. No matter how human I felt around him. Because at the end of the day, if Aspen died, I would die. And that was no life at all. So for Aspen to live, for me to live, Connor would die. He was just a vampire, anyway.

I found my bike and got on it, kicking the engine to life. I rolled out, determined to finish what I'd started. It wasn't far to Mulberry Street, and when I was at the top of the street most homes were filled with sleeping bodies. Their resting states reached out to me with long fingers that reminded me how tired I was. It wasn't the kind of tired that I could fix with sleep. This was the kind of tired that had built up in with a lifetime of doing things that never brought me peace.

When I reached number thirteen it was quiet and dark. The Jasmine in the air pinched my nose and I was annoyed with it, wishing it would go away. I killed the motor and popped out the stand, leaving the bike in the drive. I made my way into the house. It was still empty, I'd felt it the moment I'd set foot in the yard. It had been a saving grace for me earlier tonight, but now the tables were turned and he was lucky, or he'd be dead in three seconds. But he would come back eventually, and until he did I wasn't leaving.

Clyde was in the kitchen again when I walked in, and he mewed. I hopped up onto the counter and settled in the corner where the tall cabinet rose up. The cat rubbed up against my arm, purring.

"Two-face," I said softly, but scratched the cat behind his ears. It was nice to have a living being close to me. The warmth was comforting, and I felt safer than I had all night. I leaned against the tall cabinet, my head resting against the wood. My head felt heavy, suddenly, and I closed my eyes.

I jolted awake from the grating sound of shutter rolling into place. The house was locking down in anticipation of dawn. I panicked. I'd fallen asleep, and I hadn't heard a thing. Clyde was on my lap, head lolling off the side, fast asleep.

I strained my ears, trying to hear past the grating sound if someone was home, but I heard and felt nothing. The shutters were probably time-controlled. I looked at my phone. The battery was low. The time told me it would be dawn in about ten minutes.

"Are you ready to tango?" I asked Clyde, and scratched its neck softly. The cat started purring softly again, and I wondered if it would still like me after I killed its master.

The front door clicked, and I felt Connor come home before I saw him. His aura was like a sweet mist at dawn, before the sun drove it away. Fresh, unscathed, unpolluted. I wrapped my fingers around the stake at my side, and crouched, ready to lunge for him when he walked through the door.

He walked in without switching on the light which made it easier for me to stay concealed until the last moment. He heard me before I moved but I was quick enough with the element of surprise on my side. I had him up against the wall, my arm against his throat again just like before. My stake was against his skin, pushing against it. I should have done it right away, but something stopped me again.

"You promised not to bring the stake," he said softly.

"You were supposed to meet me at sunset," I countered.

"I had to take care of something and I didn't know how to contact you."

"Well, that's too bad." I pressed my arm harder against his throat. He gasped for air and his breathing was raspy. I could feel it against my arm on his throat.

"Does that deserve you trying to kill me?" he asked. He still wasn't scared.

Tears suddenly sprung to my eyes and I snarled at him through clenched teeth because he'd managed to make me cry. I never cried.

"I can't lose her, okay? If I let you live she dies." The tears streamed down my cheeks now and I felt ashamed. I pressed the stake harder against the soft skin under his ribs. He looked me in the eye, and his dark ocean-eyes looked right into my soul. Why the hell wasn't he scared of me? Didn't he believe I was going to kill him? Didn't I?

"I'll do it!" I cried out, threatening, pushing against the skin hard enough to leave a bruise. My whole body was tense, muscles aching with the strain of keeping myself together.

Connor didn't say anything. He didn't try to fight. His eyes were on me, and they were so soft I felt like I was going to break open and everything that was trapped inside was going to fall out. The atmosphere around us changed, became thick again. Thick and warm and... safe. I hadn't felt like this since I was a little girl.

"Don't do this," Connor said softly, finally talking. The atmosphere wrapped us in a cocoon, and I was suddenly aware how close our bodies were together, how gentle his eyes were with the lack of fear.

I opened my hand and the stake clattered to the floor. Slowly I eased off with my arm, and then buried my face in my hands. Connor still didn't move away from me, his warmth stayed exactly where it was. Instead he lifted his hands, both of them, and cupped my cheeks. He moved slowly, like I was a scared animal that he didn't want to startle. His face inched closer to mine, and the next thing I knew his lips came down on mine, and he kissed me.

Electricity shot through my body and my skin everywhere tingled with the sensation. The tips of his fangs were on my bottom lip, his mouth covered mine, and he reduced me to a melting mess. I wasn't a vampire hunter, who wore leather and carried guns and killed for a living. I was the damsel in distress that had been running from my hell all my life, and inwardly I was begging Connor to save me.

His kissing became urgent, his arm wrapping around my body. The gun at my back bit into my skin and the one under my jacket pushed into my ribs. I stopped Connor and pulled them both out, laying them on the counter. He raised his eyebrows.

"I see you brought back up. In case the stake didn't work?"

"Standard issue vampire-hunter kit," I said. He didn't let me keep talking. His pulled me harshly into his body and kissed me, hard. We tumbled through the house, knocking things off and banging doors until we finally made it to his bedroom. We collapsed on the bed, his body on mine, and I could feel his muscles ripple under his skin, feel his body hard and able, even though he never used it against me to save himself. He was only using it now, to save me.

He undressed me, stripping me of my holsters and sheaths until I was naked. In the almost-black room I could feel his eyes on me, tracing every inch of my body. I knew he had night vision that was better than mine and he saw me perfectly. I could smell his arousal, his lust for me in the room around us. It wrapped around me like a cloak and my body responded to him.

He lowered himself onto me, and everything was forgotten. He managed to clear my mind and work my body into a state of ecstasy, making me forget where my body ended and his began. And afterward, when everything was over and I lay in the crook of his arm, really naked without anything to define me, listening to the drum of his heart through his chest, running my forefinger over the tips of his fangs, I fell asleep. For the first time in sixteen years I didn't have a gun under my pillow.

Chapter 13

I woke up to darkness. The room around me was suffocating with it, and where the window should have been was only a vague shape of black. I sat up and looked around. Everything was different.

A movement next to me startled me, until I realized it was Connor. I wasn't in my home, I was in his. And I was in his bed, with him. Naked. I tried to orientate myself. It was Sunday, sometime, but the darkness in the house made it hard to tell what time it was. I didn't know how long I'd slept.

I slipped from underneath the covers and found my clothes on the floor, half-tangled with my holsters which were empty. I felt vulnerable without my guns. I padded to the kitchen and found them on the counter, my stake on the floor near the wall. When I found my phone, also on the floor, it was dead.

I put the guns back into their holsters, and flipped on the kitchen light. The darkness was chewing at me and I didn't want more of it. I wanted the shutters to open. I wanted to get out of the house, but I couldn't do any of it. I didn't know where or how. I'd spent a lot of my adult life breaking into vampire homes. I hadn't spent a lot of times breaking out of them.

Aspen would be worried about me. My stomach turned and an iron fist of anxiety clamped down on it when I thought about her. I would lose her if I didn't kill Connor. Why the hell hadn't I killed him? Instead I'd gone and slept with him.

Great move, Adele. Great move.

Dammit.

There weren't a lot of options. The only way was to get rid of Connor. No matter what it did to me. Because losing Aspen would do worse. There was no pain that would compare to losing her. These were facts, and it didn't matter how things were.

Connor appeared behind me before I managed to smell him or feel him. He'd crept up on me noiselessly. I spun around and pulled out my Smith & Wesson, pointing it at his head. He froze in his tracks, slowly lifting his hands.

"What are you doing?" he asked.

"What does it look like I'm doing?"

He rolled his eyes and dropped his hands. I was getting tired of him not feeling threatened by me. I had a gun this time. I could keep far enough away from his so that his body, his eyes, everything that made him Connor, wouldn't distract me.

"Are we back to that again?" he asked. "Dammit Adele, I thought we'd passed that. We just slept together, for god's sake."

I shook my head, forcing emotions down that threatened to bubble up. I could still feel his body against mine, the imprint of him between my legs. I ignored it.

"She'll die," I said, my voice so soft it didn't sound threatening at all. "Your master vampires, they're going to kill her if I don't kill you." Tears ran over my cheeks and the anger that came with it licked through my body like a wet tongue. "I can't lose her. Don't you see? There's no other way out of this."

He took a step closer to me. "Will you just let me—"

I didn't give him a chance. I fired the gun. I hadn't intended to hit him. The gun bit a hole into the concrete wall behind him, big and ugly and raw. He ducked and then turned to look at the hole.

"What the hell, Adele?" he exclaimed. "This isn't you."

"Oh no, that's where you're wrong," I said and now my voice sounded a lot more like my own. "This is exactly me. This is what I do, Connor. You can't love someone like me because I kill people like you. I kill vampires."

"Will you just calm down and we can talk about this? Maybe we can figure this out. I know them, I know what they can do. And I know what they can't."

"I know what they can do, too," I said, not taking my gun off him. He moved slowly toward the table that stood in the corner, and sat down on the chair. "They can kill Aspen."

He sighed. "I don't even know who that is. I don't know anything about you, and every time I think I've figured something out you pull the rug from underneath me."

I took a deep, shaky breath. Could I tell him? Could I trust him? I should just kill him. I knew it. But he was so casual, and leaning on his knees with his elbows the way he did now just made him look tired, even though he'd just woken up. I dropped my gun, letting it hang by my side, but my finger was still ready to slip onto the trigger. I wasn't going to let down my guard with him again. Weird things happened when I did.

"She's my sister," I said. "She's in a wheelchair, she can't fend for herself. And she's like me."

"Like you? Wild and unpredictable? Good with guns? Beautiful?"

That last comment threw me off-balance and I whipped the gun back up, pointing it at his face. I bit my bottom lip.

"Easy, easy there," Connor said, pulling his hands back up, "It was just a compliment. I was trying to keep things light. I won't mean it if you don't want me to."

A tremble ran up my arm from where my finger was on the trigger, and shook through the rest of my body.

"A half-breed," I whispered. Someone ought to know. If I died, they would know. And if he died my secret would die with him. What did I have to lose? It was a question I'd been asking myself for a long time, and I still didn't have an answer.

Connor looked like the sun had suddenly come up for him. Maybe he was thinking about the times I'd nearly managed to kill him, the way I moved but my lack of fangs.

"I've heard of half-breeds before," he said. "I just didn't know they were real. How can you kill vampires if you're half-vampire yourself?"

Wasn't that the question to ask?

"Because vampires are what put Aspen in a wheelchair, and killed my mother."

"And your father?"

"He was the vampire that did it."

He looked at me, and I could see him thinking about it. He put all the pieces together, the jail, me, my job. And then he nodded slowly.

"Tell me about Aspen," he said softly. I sighed and walked toward the table where he sat, sitting down opposite him. I put the gun down on the table, ready to grab, but the barrel didn't face him.

"She's like Christmas morning," I said. "The kind of person everyone wished they knew just by looking at her. She's thin and frail like a wisp, but she's fought through one of the hardest battles I know. People think she's weak, but she's stronger than I am."

"You're pretty strong, if you can handle all of this," he said, nodding toward the gun.

"She deals with everything I do, without killing anyone for it. She's a good person."

"Hey," Connor said and put his hand on mine. I flinched but I didn't pull it away. "You're not a bad person."

I snorted. "Now you're just trying to be nice," I said. "I kill vampires, Connor. Even though I believe they have feelings and lives and loved ones. Just because the law doesn't have a fit when some disappear the way it does with humans, does not make me a good person for doing it."

Conner sat back in his chair, taking his hand and his warmth with him, and I felt his absence acutely.

"Well, maybe you should just fix it, then," he said. "It's not too late to change."

"You should know," I said. He grinned half-heartedly and looked down at the gun that lay between us.

"You know, if I were human they would have killed me. When I found out about the trafficking I wanted to put a stop to it, but nothing is that easy."

"Police?" I asked.

"No... they would arrest me. All the paperwork is in my name. I didn't think I'd even survive a trial. My company definitely wouldn't, and I wanted to leave a legacy behind. Something my children could take over one day. But now... I don't think that's going to happen, either."

"What, your girlfriend not the vampire loving type?" I said and smiled. Jennifer was much too perfect for something like that. Connor's smile vanished when I mentioned her name.

"Not exactly. She wouldn't have me now. Besides I didn't really think she was in it for the love, anyway."

"No, rather for your money, right? Why else would she keep all that a secret?"

Connor's head shot up and his eyes were a cold kind of blue. "What did you say?"

I suddenly realized I maybe shouldn't have said something. Connor looked so hurt I wanted to kick myself. And that was saying something considering I'd been willing to kill him eight out of ten times.

"But you slept with me, so you're not really in a good place to beg for her mercy right now," I said lightly, trying to change the topic.

"She kept what secret?" Connor asked, narrowing his eyes at me. He was like a dog that had bitten into something and wouldn't let go now.

"I don't think..." I started but his face stopped me. Anger and hatred poured out of him in waves that smelled rotten. I wondered for a second if this was what I looked like to other people. Suddenly his hand scooped up the gun so fast I couldn't react quickly enough, and before I knew it he was pointing it at my head.

One thing I suddenly realized was that the business end of my gun was not the end I wanted to be on.

"Now, don't do anything rash," I said calmly. Connor had stood up and I pushed myself up too, moving slowly so he wouldn't do anything stupid. The gun burned me where it pointed at my skin. Right at my heart. Something told me Connor had worked with fire arms before.

"You do this all the time, don't you?" Connor said. "I kind of see the appeal."

"You don't mean that," I said, still keeping my voice calm. "This is just a misunderstanding. You knew Jennifer sent me. I was just on the wrong tangent." I would say anything to him until I was on the other side of that gun.

"Tell me what you know," he said.

"I don't know anything—"I started but his finger curled around the trigger and I knew I was running out of time.

"I found out she knew more about the trafficking than she let on, but other than that I don't know anything. I went to confront her for lying to me after I found your article, and I left when I couldn't stand being around her anymore."

"She knew about it? Why did she keep it quiet from me?"

"Because she said..." I swallowed hard. I hated being the one that ruined the image of a loved one. I knew what that did to someone. "She said it was because she needed you to marry her. She couldn't go back to the hole her ex had left her in."

His face fell and his attention wasn't on me for two seconds. If I moved now maybe I could get the gun away from him and swing it all around again so that I was in charge. But his eyes slid back to me. "Her ex. It always comes back down to that. I'm so sick of hearing how I compare, how her life is exponentially better because of me when at the end of the day I know it's just about money."

I groaned inwardly. I didn't like having a gun on me. I didn't like emotionally unstable people. I didn't like monologues and I didn't like it when someone made their problems mine.

"Look, just put the gun down, okay? Your drama is between you two. All I was doing was finishing a job."

"Who's job, hers or the masters'?" he asked.

I didn't think about it. I didn't take the time. I'd been distracting him with conversation, and now that he was in a puddle of confusion I made my move. I was in his face before he knew it, and I snatched the gun out of his hand. I pressed it against his chest, and squeezed the trigger. The clap of the bullet was loud and tiles splintered against the wall behind Connor. And he was gone.

A thick black mist hung in the air and I sank into a squat to get away from it, but Connor had dematerialized faster than my finger had been on the trigger.

Where had he gone to in the middle of the day? It didn't matter. He was still alive, which meant I had to get to Aspen.

I found the electrical box and flung it open. I didn't know anything about fuses and switches, so I took my blade and cut through the whole lot of wires in front of me. The shutters slid open and all the lights went out. I walked out the front door into bright sunlight, and got on my bike.

It took me all of five minutes to get to Aspen's neighborhood and knock on the door. When Zelda opened she blinked at me, surprised.

"Oh, Adele. It's you. We weren't expecting you," she said, glancing over my shoulder.

"Who were you expecting?"

"Aspen is expecting a Mr. Joel."

Joel was coming by? I pushed passed Zelda and walked into the house. Aspen was in the dining room at a table, setting out a tray with mugs for coffee.

"Adele! Where have you been? I tried calling but I only got voicemail and I know you never check those."

"I'm sorry, I've been busy. Are you alright?" I walked to the wall and plugged my phone in to charge.

"I'm fine," she said, smiling at me. "Joel's coming over."

"Why?"

"He contacted me yesterday and asked if he could set up the cameras you asked for."

The cameras I'd asked for? I kept the questions off my face. He was a hell of a friend.

"I'm so glad he's coming," I said and the relief was complete when it washed through me. It was a way I could keep her safe until I found Connor. I had no idea what had just happened between us, but I was pretty sure he wasn't just going to show up any time soon after that.

"What's wrong?" Aspen asked. I didn't know what my face showed, but I cleared it.

"Nothing," I said. "When is he coming?"

"Any minute. Zelda thought it was him when the doorbell rang."

I sat down and we waited together after I borrowed a charger and plugged in my phone.

"How's your case coming along?" Aspen asked.

"My case?" I had to make a point of keep track of my lies with her, I told myself.

"The one where you were looking for the guy that was kidnapped."

"Oh." That one. The one where that guy and I had slept together and now wanted to kill each other. "He's a vampire, after all. A lot of people are after him."

"I'm sorry," Aspen said, reaching over and putting her hand on mine.

"It's okay. He's different than the rest. I hope for his sake they find him, because I don't want to."

Aspen didn't answer and when I looked up at her she was smiling.

"What?"

"You smell like frustration," she said. "Frustration and sex."

"I do not!" I cried out. "You're being inappropriate."

"You slept with someone! You slept with someone and now you're angry. You like him, don't you? Only men make you this angry."

"I don't like anyone. In fact, there are some people I hate all the more now."

Aspen smiled, dropping the topic, but she gave me a knowing look. I rolled my eyes. I didn't like anyone. Besides, if I liked Connor I wouldn't have nearly blown a hole in his chest, would I have? Aspen was being absurd.

We talked about other things. I asked about her week. It felt like I hadn't seen her in a while. The time ticked by, and after an hour had passed I frowned.

"He's running very late," I said. Joel was never late.

"Do you think something came up?"

I shook my head and walked to my phone. I dialed Joel's number, but it went straight to voicemail. Joel's phone was never off. If he couldn't be connected he lost his mind.

"I'm going to take a drive," I said. The blood in my veins tingled, and I felt like an itch crept in under my skin. I'd been around the block enough times to know that I shouldn't ignore this feeling. I stopped at the door.

"I want you to get out of here," I said to Aspen.

"To go where?"

"To a safe house," I said. I took a deep breath, bracing myself for my own words. "To mom's house."

"But…" her voice trailed off. We'd never gotten rid of the house. I couldn't let it go. It was like I was letting mom go, then.

"Trust me, Aspen. It's not safe for you. I've been working on… a case. And they guys are making this personal. I don't want to lose you."

When I looked at her, her face was contorted with horror.

"I don't want you to be afraid. I'm keeping you safe before things get out of hand. But this one will get worse before it gets better, and I can't risk you getting in the crossfire."

"Adele…" Aspen's voice was soft and she looked down at the hands in her lap. "You're not a cop, are you?"

I hesitated before I shook my head slowly. When she looked up at me her eyes were shimmering and tears welled up in them. How long had she been pretending she believed me for my sake? We both knew she wasn't stupid and we'd both been pretending.

"Promise me one thing," she said. "One thing and I'll go."

"What is it?"

"After this you'll put to rest all the demons that are still chasing you."

I took a deep breath and blew it out in a shudder.

"I don't know if I can do that."

"Promise you'll try?" she asked. And I nodded. Because for Aspen I would do anything. For Aspen I would change the world.

"Get your bags packed," I said, and Zelda jumped into action. I walked over to Aspen and hugged her. She wrapped her arms around me. I squeezed my eyes shut, regretting what I was about to do. I bit her in the neck.

Aspen jerked and shoved me away hard enough for her wheelchair to move back despite the breaks. Her hand went to her neck and when she pulled it away it was red.

"What the hell?" she cried out. With blunt teeth the bite was a hell of a lot harder because I had to break the skin. The metallic taste of her blood was in my mouth. "You bit me!"

"I'm sorry," I said.

"Who are you, Adele? You're not the person I used to know, anymore. You've changed."

I sighed. I had, she was right. But hearing it from her hurt more than my own admittance to the truth.

"You have to get to the house as fast as you can. I'll meet you there as soon as I have some kind of lead on Joel."

I turned and walked out.

Chapter 14

When I pulled in front of Joel's house there was nothing left of it. The entire place had been burned to the ground, a charred mark shaping out the floor plan and singed rubble lying in heaps all over the place. This hadn't been done by human hands. Humans couldn't burn a place like this, so that there was virtually nothing left. Not even walls.

I knew who'd done this. Some master vampires had fire as their ability. And most of them were destructive. This was past a warning. This was their first move.

I walked onto the property and stood where the garage used to be. The sun was sinking behind the horizon, casting long creepy shadows across the ground, making the burned lot seem so much more morbid. Any other regular family would be spending a Sunday evening inside with the family. I was the only that was out on a rest day, trying to do some form of chaos control. I could feel the people in the neighborhood around me, calm, peaceful, content if not overly happy. I was suddenly jealous.

I kicked around a bit, ash flying up into the air in a grey cloud. My toe stubbed against a latch, and I scraped away the ash with my foot to reveal the trap door that led down to the pit.

When I opened the door, the stairs that led into the ground weren't blackened and charred like the rest of the place. The fire hadn't gotten this far. It had served its intended use as a bomb shelter after all.

I stepped into the darkness, and flicked the switch. The hum of the generator kicking in filled the air around me, and the pit lit up in a light-green flicker.

It looked a lot like it had on the video Joel had shown me when we'd met after Celia had trashed his place. But it wasn't quite the same. Then it had looked like someone had left a warning. Now it looked like someone had fought for their life.

A splatter of blood against the far wall drew my attention. There were more smears on the floor. I inhaled deeply, and recognized Joel straight away. He'd been hurt here, bleeding. There was no more blood than this.

He was still alive unless they'd killed him somewhere else. And I had to find him.

I rummaged through the rubble, looking for something, anything, that I could use to find a lead on him. There were a lot of papers lying around, most of them with information and data on it that I didn't understand. His filing system was shot to hell, and all the gun cabinets and safes were thrown open. If there had been any weapons and ammunition, it had been taken.

But I still didn't get the feeling they'd been here to gain from his belongings. They were interested only and Joel. And that was because of his involvement with me.

My stomach turned and guilt swirled around like nausea. A bitter taste in the back of my throat told me what I didn't want to know. This was all my fault. If people died here, their blood would be on my hands.

As a killer that shouldn't have bothered me. But it did, because Joel was a friend. And Aspen... I took a deep breath. I couldn't even bring myself to imagine what it would be like to lose her. There would be nothing left in my life, no reason why I was doing any of this.

My hands grazed something hard underneath the papers I'd been fishing through, and I found a laptop. It looked like it had been caught in the fire. Which mean t it had been upstairs when the fire had started, and someone had moved it down here afterwards.

Joel?

To me that meant that there was something on it that was important. That he didn't want to lose in the fire. Joel uploaded everything he had onto back up servers that were protected and out of the way. Whatever it was he wanted to protect wasn't in the cloud of data online. It was only on this laptop.

I tucked the laptop under my arm.

When I turned she was standing at the bottom of the stairs. Her white hair caught the light streaming in through the trapdoor, and it looked like silk. She was smiling but her green eyes didn't reflect any kind of emotion other than cold hatred.

"Can Adele come out and play?" she said in a mocking voice. I rolled my eyes.

"Not today, princess."

She scowled. I carried on looking through the pit, pretending to ignore her, but I kept my attention on her. She didn't move, although I could feel contempt radiating off her in waves. She didn't like being ignored. I kept moving, trying to mask the nerves that were bunching at the bottom of my throat, clenching my stomach.

She took a deep breath through her nose, and then she cackled a laugh.

"You're scared of me," she said.

Well, yes. I was. Because I hadn't been able to defeat her. I hadn't been able to make any kind of progress on knowing how to get to her. And the memories of the previous fights with her, where I'd lost horribly, were too fresh in my mind. But I put on an emotionless smile of my own.

"Being fearless is reckless. You have nothing to gain. I do." I was talking about love. About emotion, about having something left in life that wasn't materialistic. That wasn't based on achievements. I didn't think she understood something like that.

"Well, if you wait long enough, you won't have anything to gain, either. The difference between you and me is that I have nothing left to *lose*, either. You, on the other hand, still do. And your time's running out."

I lost my cool. I could only put on a face for so long. I put the laptop casually on a table, and turned to face her as calmly as I could force myself to be. I launched for her, faster and stronger than I'd been before. Fear and anger were a deadly combination if you applied them right. She laughed in a cackle again that danced around me, singing in my head, echoing through my hollow bones. She was quicker than I was, standing where'd I'd stood before I reached her.

I turned and looked at her. She dragged a long black nail over the laptop. I wondered if she'd had those nails in the interview with Ruben, or if she could retract them like claws. When she smiled I realized she could take away the only lead I might have. I attacked again without thinking. This time I reached her before she had a chance to move and I managed to hit her in the face, a strong blow to the jaw. She stumbled backward and I got between her and the laptop.

She hissed at me, eyes flashing rage.

Then she disappeared, moving around me in a blur and out of the door, the image of her fading long after she'd left. A cold feeling stayed behind, like frost that licked up my body. I shivered, and the nerves I'd felt before solidified and became a rock of terror in my stomach. She *did* know what I was talking about. And I was about to lose someone if I didn't make a plan soon.

Joel was my techy. He was the one I would have run to with this laptop to find a way to hack out the information. I had no idea where else to go. So I took out my phone and I did the one thing I didn't ever in my life think I would do.

I phoned Carl.

"Listen, I need a favor," I said into the speaker when he answered sounding as crisp as ever. Didn't this man ever sleep? The only reason I was up and running was because life threatening events tended to pump adrenaline into me. Otherwise I would have been home and in bed too. I thought about bed and thought of Connor's house. I pushed the memories away.

Maybe Carl had a hell of a life too. Who knew what turned someone to a gun for a living?

"Oh, the great Adele Griffin comes to me. What did I do to deserve this honor?" The sarcasm bled through his words.

"Can it, Carl. I need help and it's urgent."

He groaned into the phone. "What do you want?"

"A technician that will help me crack a laptop that's been… damaged." I turned the piece of scrap around in my hands. That's all description I had left for this thing.

"What happened to yours?"

"It was in a fire."

"Your technician?"

Well, yeah, but that was not what I wanted him to know. "The laptop."

Carl chuckled like it was a joke.

"Don't you know someone? People are going to die if I can't crack this thing."

Carl whistled through his teeth. "Sounds like you've been getting some action. Better than me, I've been hitting a dry spell for far too long."

I tried not to imagine what he meant by that.

"I'll give it to you on one condition," he said.

"What?"

"I want in on whatever it is you're doing."

"Are you crazy?"

He took a deep breath. "There are days I think I might be," he said and his voice was so sincere I had the feeling he wasn't joking this time.

"Fine," I said. I needed it, I couldn't turn him down now or Joel might die. If I was still alive he could get in on the action. I'd already sacrificed enough people. Why not another one I could kill myself over? Right.

He gave me the number of a guy. "Used him a couple of times. He's good, knows what he does. He should have some time for you too, his busy time is at night."

So, more technicians had the wrong friends. It was calming somehow to know this guy wasn't straightforward vanilla. Maybe he wouldn't chase me away with my leathers and guns.

"Thanks," I said to Carl and hung up before he could say anything out of line.

I phoned the guy. His voice was gravelly over the phone, like he was talking to me through a sieve, and he sounded weary. After a bit of smooth talking I finally got him to agree to taking on a client he didn't know. I guessed in his line of work being cautious could save your life. I felt the same way about strangers so I could respect that.

I got an address and a meeting for eight tomorrow morning. My week was going to start with a bang. He'd had openings for tonight, but I had a rule about going to meet people in the middle of the night. I'd killed enough under the cloak of darkness to know I didn't want to be the one that ended up on the other end of that food chain.

The only thing left for me to do now was to go home. I took a deep breath and blew it out in a shudder. I didn't want to leave Joel to fend for himself alone, but I didn't have much of a choice. I would be no good to him if I were dead – I had to take care of myself first.

My apartment was cold and dark when I arrived. I didn't usually spend nighttime indoors. I was a nocturnal creature and the walls felt like they were closing down on me and suffocating me. I opened the curtains so I could see the inky black air with the pinpricks of stars stretching across it like a blanket.

I stripped of my leathers and took a shower. I had the knife with me permanently now. The whole apartment looked different in the yellow light that replaced sunlight, and I didn't feel like I was at my own home. When I crawled into bed I fell asleep straight away, but sometimes that wasn't enough for me to escape my life.

I had nightmares about Joel, burning alive, throwing his laptop out at me, yelling for me to get to Aspen before she burned too. The sounds of bullets splintering tiles came out of his mouth every time he called for me.

I tried to get to Aspen but hot black tar stopped my bike's wheels from turning. When I got off and tried to run my feet sucked into it and I had to fight for every step.

When I finally got to Aspen's house it was dark, and Zelda was there, beckoning me into the black. Aspen's voice called out to me, clear and crystal as always, music in the night. I couldn't see anything but I followed the sound of her voice, feeling around for her in the dark. Flames started licking around us, consuming the house, lighting up the place enough for me to see. I found Aspen and wrapped my arms around her frail body, but she felt stronger and firmer than usual. When I pulled away again it was Connor staring back at me.

"Where's Aspen?" I asked him, drawing back. I didn't want to touch him. The warmth that flowed from him threatened to suck me in, and my memories of Aspen slipped away from me like bathwater down a drain.

"She's right there," he said, pointing at someone behind me. When I spun around it was Celia standing behind me. Her hair was white, her eyes a brilliant green. When I looked at Connor again, frowning, he looked like her too. They both laughed and their cackling surrounded me like a storm.

I sat up, the darkness in my room folding around me. The nightmare slowly faded, but my heart hammered in my chest and I was hyperventilating. I swung my legs off the bed and leaned my head down between my knees. I focused on getting my breathing back to normal.

When I looked up again the night sky had a silvery quality to it, anticipating dawn. Thank god.

I got up and climbed in the shower again. I turned on only the hot water and I stood underneath the scalding stream. The drops hit my skin like a thousand needles. I ignored the pain on my leg. The graze was a lot smaller but still there. At least it didn't bother me anymore, not like before. Steam fogged up the entire bathroom, hanging in the air like fog, an artificial sky, and I couldn't breathe in the humidity. But at least through all the pain and discomfort I knew I was alive. I was back in reality.

I got into running clothes, found my chain, and stepped out of my apartment. The hallways and the lobby smelled dusty and moldy, and I wondered how I'd survived in this place for so long. When I finally stepped into the crisp morning air I took a deep breath, and ran.

I ran until my muscles screamed at me, until my legs felt numb and my chest burned every time I took a breath. My neck and shoulders were rubbed numb with the weight of the chain. I ran until I couldn't run anymore, and then I turned around and started the run home.

Finally it rolled onto seven-thirty. I got dressed into my leathers and suited up. My knife in the thigh sheath, my S&W in my shoulder holster under my jacket, my SIG at my back. I glanced at the Carbine but decided against it. I needed Carlos to let me in. I did make sure I had the black chain in the bike's compartment, though. Just in case. I always fell back onto my saying – luck favored the prepared.

I got on my bike and navigated the streets of town. He was a couple of blocks away from my own place, but in an even worse part of town. I hadn't been sure that was possible at all. The street looked like the garbage removal just skipped it on garbage day, and there weren't even stray cats around. If the cats didn't bother, you had to know.

I found the apartment he'd described and buzzed the first intercom on the list. None of them were marked. The wind picked up and a chilly finger sliced through me, despite the leathers. It was the kind of cold that came with foreboding.

The door buzzed open and I stepped into an apartment building that looked like it had been abandoned decades ago. The decorations inside were old, the wallpapers seemed like golden floral print under the dust and the carpet was once a deep red. I could see this on the few patches that weren't worn down to the concrete beneath. It, too, was dusty.

A chandelier hung from the ceiling with real candles in it, all burned down to a pile of wax and black quick, and the elevator behind it still had a steel gate in front of the wooden door that closed it.

I walked past reception where a visitor's book was open and signed here and there with curly handwriting, but there was no doorman. Not physically anyway. The presence that hung in the lobby made me wonder if he still hung around from time to time, checking in from the afterlife.

I knocked on the first door on the ground floor, a white door that looked used and lacked cobwebs, unlike the others. Two seconds later the door opened.

A man stood in front of me with long hair that hung in greasy strings around his face. He was clean shaven but he had a slimy quality about him. His shirt had grease stains all the way down the front, wrapping around a body that he obviously maintained with fast foods, and his eyes were a watered down grey.

"Carlos Sanchez?" I asked and he nodded. "I'm Adele Griffin."

"Come on in," he said, opening the door wider. The inside of his apartment was a staggering contrast to the horrible neighborhood and the exterior of the rest of the building. He had plush grey carpets and salmon colored walls, with high tech equipment on a desk in the corner and a wide screen television against the wall. It looked and smelled like it was all cleaned half an hour ago.

"Do you want coffee?" he asked, walking into the kitchen.

"I'm okay," I said. I wasn't sure what to expect in the cup. Better not to expect anything. He came out with one cup of coffee with the steam curling out of it, the aroma wrapping around the room and reminding me suddenly of home – when I was little and Aspen and I would watch my dad make breakfast-in-bed for my mom. The reminder was so strong I felt like I was shoved backward.

"What do you have for me?" he said, nodding to the laptop under my arm and yanking me back to the presence.

I handed it over to him. "I think it's been in a fire. I just need to know why someone wanted to save it. I think there's something on there that might be important."

He looked at it, lifting his eyebrows.

"Well, if we get something out of it we'll be lucky, but I can have a look," he said. We moved to his desk in the corner and he sat down. I perched on the edge of the armchair nearby.

He unscrewed it and pulled out the insides. He found a green plate-like thing and turned it over in his hands like it could break under his gaze.

"Well, this survived a lot better than expected," he said. "Let's have a look."

He hooked it up to a silver box with wires and his fingers flew over his keyboard the same Joel's usually did. I wondered if they were all the same, how they got into this line of work, what made then stray away from the daily grind where none of them would have to worry about being kidnapped or burned to death.

It took him a while, but after ten minutes he swiveled his chair to face me.

"Okay, so it looks like the standard stuff for the most part. Nothing I'd say I would be killed over if it were me. But there is one thing here..."

I leaned forward. "What is it?"

"A tracking system. It's been installed two days ago on this laptop."

"What is it tracking?"

"It's not tracking anymore, but I can tell you where it was pointing the last time it worked."

He squinted at the screen, and read me the address. It was Aspen's house.

Relief spread through my body like warm liquid and I slipped down to the seat of the armchair. "Thank god," I said out loud. "He was watching her after all."

"Someone you know?" he asked. I nodded and he carried on. "Yes, someone close, I gather. People don't watch over those they don't care about. Well, there's something you should know."

I looked up at him.

"I know this system, because I installed a very similar one a day ago for someone."

"Okay..." I didn't feel like a tech heart to heart. I wanted to interrupt, but he kept talking.

"The address for it was the same one."

It took me two seconds to register what he was saying before my body went cold. Blood drained from my face and I felt like I had to put my head between my knees if I didn't want to faint.

"It's them, isn't it?" I whispered.

"If by them you mean—"

"Master vampires," I finished for him. He nodded grimly.

"They want to kill her."

"They didn't look like the kind that were doing it for fun," he agreed.

"They won't find her though. She's not at that address anymore." It was a small consolation, but right now it meant the difference between life and death for her. "Why did you do it for them? If you knew they didn't look like they had good intentions?"

Carlos swiveled to face me dead on.

"They offered me more money than I make in a year. I have standards... but for that kind of money?" He shrugged. "What I can do for you, though, and I'll throw this one in free of charge, is look up the tracker location."

I frowned. "On *their* system? You can do that?" I asked.

"Well I installed it, didn't I? I can hack in and check the system. I set up the firewalls in the first place."

He typed in a couple of commands, and a moment later a screen popped up. It had a map of the town and a round loading icon.

"It should give me the address," he said. "Just give me a min—ah hah. Here we are."

He looked at the map with a red blinking dot on it. I got up and leaned in closer. The dot blinked steadily in one spot, it wasn't moving. But it wasn't at Aspen's house either. It was at the safe house.

"This is right?" I asked. Carlos looked at me indignantly.

"I wouldn't charge this much if—"

"Just tell me if it's right, dammit!" I yelled. His face became stony but he nodded.

I spun and ran out the door.

"You owe me money!" he shouted after me.

"I'll pay you later," I answered, running through the dusty lobby and out into the sunlight where I'd parked my bike.

Chapter 15

There were times when I'd felt Westham was too small for me. Too small for my bike. Too small for my life. I wanted a place that was bigger, that I could get lost in, with so many faces that I no one would end up knowing me anymore.

And then there were days like today, when it felt like forever to navigate the streets of the small town. I opened my bike full throttle where I could, but it felt like I was moving in slow motion. I could hear my own pulse thundering in my ears, felt it in the tips of my fingers where they curled around the throttle.

I still heard the cackling laugh of Celia the Werecat dancing around me in Joel's pit. I tried to breathe, forced myself to take a deep breath, and another, and another. But my chest was tight and my body did nothing with the oxygen.

I skidded to a halt outside my childhood home. It was like a horror movie. The oak tree to the side of the drive way had grown since I'd last seen it. Leaves were scattered on the grass even though it had been cut recently. The low roof over the porch looked like it was drawing over the house, forcing it to squat down on itself.

I wondered if it was because of my panic now that this place looked like it was suffocating, or if it had always been like that and as a child I just hadn't noticed.

Claude's car stood in the driveway to the side of the house. It was unlocked. I opened the door expecting the worse, but there was nothing. No blood, no sign of struggle. No Aspen. I ran my hand under the cover under the steering wheel in the foot well. I checked under the passenger seat. There was nothing there, no tracker I could find, and I didn't have the time to keep looking. It didn't matter. The tracker said they had to be here.

I ran up to the front door and tried the handle. The door was locked. I rattled it, yelling for Aspen. Great approach when expecting master vampires. In my distress I was getting careless, but there was a point for every person where action replaced logic. When there was no response I ran around the back and hopped the low gate. The concrete in the backyard was cracked with weeds growing from it, and the grass was wheat beige even though it shouldn't have been. I pressed my face against a window, cupping it with my hands so I could see into the kitchen.

Everything inside was undisturbed. The table in the corner with four seats looked ready for someone's next meal. The stove was spotless, besides the pointers of time that had passed. The microwave and the fridge missed their indicator lights showing that there was power.

A thin veil of dust lay over everything like blanket. No one had been inside.

"Aspen!" I called out. My voice felt empty as it reached only a few feet ahead of me before it disappeared. I shivered, feeling cold despite my leathers.

I ran to my bike, but halfway I slowed down. I had bitten her. Her blood was in my system. I was being stupid running around like a headless chicken. I stepped to the side and sat down on the grass under the oak tree. The leaves crackled under my weight. I took a deep breath, closed my eyes, and turned my focus inside.

I'd never done this before, I'd only heard about it from my parents. But I knew it was possible, my vampire side allowed it. I focused on my heart, slowing it down. I evened out my breathing, inhaling slowly, taking twice as long on the exhale.

The amount of blood that had been on my lips had only been a few drops. Barely anything at all. But dimly something inside me lurked, and I could feel her. She was alive.

Something inside me jumped at the knowledge. There was still time.

I focused on the faint pulse that came from her, beating in its own rhythm. I felt her emotions, dim and distant, like I was looking through fog, but it was there. She was panicked and scared, and her body was sore from being man-handled. But she was alive and she wasn't hurt.

I tried to find her. Her blood should have called out to me and told me where she was. But something blocked that quality. It was like a metal wall fell into place, and I lost the dim trail I'd picked up. Someone was hiding her, and knew how to do it on a different level. I got up, frustrated. My panic flared up again, my heart starting its wild race all over again. I ran to my bike, back into full-on panic mode.

My phone chirped in my pocket and I pulled it out. The message was from Sensei. I was late for our class. I dialed his number and waited for him to pick up on the fourth ring.

"I'm sorry, I didn't keep track of the time," I said when he answered. "I'm going to have to take a rain check today. Something's come up. I'll see you again tomorrow."

I wanted to hang up but Sensei's voice stopped me.

"I have an opening for you at two," he said. He never had openings in the afternoon, he had school runs where he taught kids self-defense for some anti-bully motion.

"I'm sorry, I don't think I'm going to be able—"

"Even if it is just for ten minutes. I just want to chat."

I opened my mouth to respond, but I didn't say anything for a moment. He wanted to talk? About what? I shook my head more to myself than to him.

"I'm sorry. It's really a wild day. I'll talk to you tomorrow," I said.

"Be careful, Adele. I worry about you."

I hung up before he could say anything else. He didn't know what my life was like. There were so many people that said 'be careful' but they didn't understand that I was *way* past that.

I was murderous.

I made it to Aspen's house in under five minutes. I was sure I'd broken every traffic rule in the book. I kicked out the bike stand and nearly dropped the whole thing to the floor before I balanced it and ran up the steps. The front door was ajar. I pushed it open carefully, and stepped inside the house.

There was sign of struggle here. End tables were on their sides, a potted plant lay on the floor with dirt scattered across the carpet. Broken pieces of glass that used to be coffee cups lay scattered toward the kitchen. When I stepped onto the tiles the smell hit me before I saw it.

Death had a smell. Rotten, a little sour, like it was something off, even though the body hadn't begun decomposing yet. And the fear often hung in the air around it, still. It took a while before it disappeared. It laced everything in the air now, and I felt nauseous before I saw her.

Zelda lay face down on the kitchen tiles, her eyes vacantly staring at the pool of dark blood that swelled around her head. The tips of her hair that had escaped from her neat bun were a wine color, stained by it. Her right arm was stretched up, like she'd been reaching for something. One blind was open, which they never were in daylight, letting the harsh sunlight in to reveal everything's true colors.

From the looks of it Zelda had run to open the blinds and only made it to one of them. If that had been the case it had been for sunlight, which meant the masters had been here. In daylight. I kneeled next to her and examined her without touching her. The blood came from a hole in her neck where her throat should have been. It was a mangled, bloody mess now. She'd been bitten and her throat ripped out to stop her. From the looks of things they hadn't taken her blood, or at least not a lot of it.

"Dear woman," I said softly. Zelda had been hard and strict, but I'd known her for a long time and she'd been good to Aspen.

I took a deep breath and tried to calm the nerves that were tangling me up inside. I had to keep my head about me. I couldn't afford to lose it now. The amount I was panicking was already dangerous.

I doubted they'd killed Aspen. They still needed me to take out Connor. If they'd already gotten to him Aspen would have been here too, dead next to Zelda. And Claude's car wouldn't have been at the safe house. No, I believed Aspen was still alive. I *needed* to believe it. They were using her for motivation, because they knew that if she died I would give up. I had to find her.

I stood up and systematically combed through the rest of the house, but nothing was out of place. The struggle had taken place between the front door and the kitchen, and it had happened quickly and without wasting a lot of time.

When I stepped out into the sunlight again it felt foreign, like the whole world was suddenly a place I didn't know. I took a deep breath through my nose and blew it out again through my mouth. The sun was high in the sky. It was rolling on towards noon and I still hadn't eaten. I felt empty and hollow, but food couldn't fill this kind of hole in my soul.

My phone rang in my pocket and I pulled it out and pushed 'talk'.

"You better get into the office," Carl's voice came loud and clear through the speaker.

"Just because I turned to you for help doesn't mean we're friends, Carl," I sneered. I didn't feel like his games. I already felt like I owed him one, and I didn't like owing people.

"Thanks for the sentiment, but don't flatter yourself," he said sarcastically. "But this is actually important. Get here. I'm guessing you can make more of this than I can, seeing that Ruben actually tells you things once in a while."

I frowned but agreed.

"I'll be there in ten. I have nothing better to do with my time."
I hung up. I'd meant that last bit sarcastically, but I realized
suddenly it was true. I had nothing. No lead on Joel, a locked-
down lead on Aspen, a cancelled appointment with Sensei, a
dead care taker and a missing driver.

Nope, I could still fit more on my plate. My bike roared into
the quiet Monday morning.

The office was quiet, which was strange. Ruben ran a normal
accounting firm in the day which meant there had to be cars
outside. There weren't. All the lights in the lobby were off, and
everything had an eerie feel to it despite the sunlight that filtered
in through the windows. The day receptionist's desk was empty.

"Carl?" I called into the quiet building. He appeared at the
top of the stairs. He looked like he'd aged since I'd last seen him.
His face was sagging, dark rings under his eyes and the blue irises
were darker, like the ocean instead of like ice.

"What's going on?" I asked, climbing the stairs to him.
"Where is everybody?"

"I don't know," he answered and for once he didn't sound
belittling or mocking or sarcastic. That in itself was more
alarming than anything else.

"Sony paged me and I came here—"

"You still use a pager?" I asked him. He rolled his eyes.

"Focus, Adele," he snapped. "Sonya paged me, which isn't that
weird – she works funny hours for a vampire – but when I got
here the whole place was quiet, like this. I hadn't been able to
come in right away so I didn't know if this had happened before
or after... So I phoned you because you know more about this
place than I do."

"Aren't you in Ruben's back pocket?" I asked. I'd always
gotten the idea Carl was the favorite. But he shook his head.

"Honestly? I think he was just doing me a favor by taking me
on. I have skills, sure. But what can I do? I'm just a human."

"Very humbling words, Carl," I said. "I always thought you were a bit of an ass—"

We'd stopped at the doors that led to Sonya's office, and what I saw cut me short. The place was a mess. The desk was upside down, a cabinet lay face down and papers were scattered all over the place. There was blood on the carpet. When I looked up the light bulbs in all the lamps that hung from the ceiling were broken.

"What the hell happened here?" I asked.

"That's what I was hoping you would tell me," Carl said, not sounding in the least offended that I was about to call him an asshole. In fact, he sounded worn. When I looked at him he looked like he was dead on his feet.

I walked through the office, looking around. Someone had been looking for something, from what I could gather, but it was such a mess it would take days, and Sonya, to know what had gone missing. I pushed against the door to Ruben's office.

"Don't go in there," Carl said. I looked over my shoulder at him and he was white as a ghost. I frowned but pushed into the office anyway. I didn't really follow orders very well.

Something leaned against the door and I had to shove to get it wide enough for me to get in there. When I managed to slip through, the door closed again, and I was trapped in the office.

There was blood everywhere, on the walls, on the carpet, papers stained. And the office was in the same mess the other one had been. The furniture was all overturned and cabinets had drawers pulled out of them with papers spilling out like secrets. When I turned to see what had stopped the door from opening, I gagged.

It was Ruben. And he was very dead.

His face was a bloody mess, like he'd been hit a couple of times. He had gashes across his body oozing blood, and his clothes were a red stained mess. His eyes were open, staring with a glazed gaze at his office. His throat was gone, worse than

Zelda's. I closed my eyes and turned my head away. The blinds all around the office were closed. The light bulbs here were broken too.

I pulled the door open, shoving against the dead body I didn't want to touch so I could get out again. When I stood in Sonya's office, I shivered, my fingers trembling. Carl was sitting on the edge of a tipped cabinet, looking small despite his bulk of muscle.

"Told you," he said, but the joking tone in his voice was missing and he looked about as haunted as I felt.

"Well," was all I could say. Carl nodded.

"Do you know what's going on here?" he asked me after a moment of silence. I nodded and walked to the cabinet, sitting down next to him. It was strange sharing personal space with someone. I was aware of the warmth that came from him, the smell of his cologne that filtered through the sour smell of death and fear, the metallic smell of blood.

"He took on the wrong clients," I said. "They're vampires, after someone for a big deal. They came to him and he took the job for the money. But it ended up costing a lot more than that."

Carl chuckled without feeling. "I'm assuming you got the job?"

I nodded. I wish I'd never taken it. "You think it's just another kill, and before you know it everyone around you is dying." I stopped talking because a lump had suddenly risen in my throat and I didn't want to cry in front of Carl.

"You know, I took this job because I wanted to prove myself to my father. Because he said I didn't have it in me, I was too soft, I'd never be a real man."

I looked at him. Underneath his charming I-don't-care façade and bulky muscles he was just a boy. He looked vulnerable now, with the events of the morning peeling away his mucho veneer.

"This doesn't make me a man, though. You know? It just makes me a murderer."

"They're vampires, Carl," I said, trying to sound like they didn't matter. But somewhere along the line I'd started to feel like they did matter. Connor mattered. And mom mattered. I sighed. "I hate it too."

"Why are you still doing it?" Carl asked.

I shrugged. "I guess when you give so much of yourself away to do it in the first place, you can't stop. There won't be anything left. This has started to define me, I guess. Why do you still do it?"

Carl shrugged, too. "Well, I think it's safe to take this as an opportunity to change jobs. The cross-over shouldn't be too hard now. No month of notice, you know?"

His attempt at a joke fell on the floor in front of us. Neither of us thought it was funny.

"So these vampires that killed him, are they after you too?" he asked.

"Yes, but not to kill me. They want me to take out the mark. They're willing to kill to make sure that happens."

"Why don't they do it themselves?"

"Because he's slippery and they lost control of their own mess. Now they're just making a mess for everyone else."

Carl nodded slowly, turning it over in his mind. "Hey, at least your life isn't in danger," he said.

"My sister's is. And my technician. If they're still alive I have to finish the job to save them. If they're already dead, well, then they've successfully killed me too."

Carl whistled through his teeth. "I can help you find him," he said. "I'm sure when we put two heads together we can do more than each of us alone can manage."

I shook my head. "It's not that easy. The mark... Connor... he's not really the kind of vampire I want to kill. He's..."

I took a deep breath, nothing finishing my sentence. Carl narrowed his eyes at me.

"I'm guessing there's a lot more to this story. Let me see what I have so far. You don't want to kill the mark because, and I'm just guessing, you have feelings for him."

"I do not," I said meekly, which was an answer in itself.

"Right. Sure. Your sister and technician are being held hostage—"

"Maybe."

"—and you need to put an end to all of this. What am I missing?"

I sighed. What did I have to lose at this point, telling him?

"My sister's care taker has been killed, my driver is missing, they have a pet cat-woman that's out to torture me within an inch of my life, and I don't know where to find Connor even if I don't want to kill him, because I shot him."

Carl raised his eyebrows.

"I missed," I answered his unasked question.

"You?"

I snorted. "Hard to believe. I know."

"These vampires... they're the ones that killed Ruben?" he swallowed hard, like the words in his mouth made him sick.

I nodded.

"And they're the ones that hired you."

"To kill him, yes. His girlfriend hired me to find him for her. At least, that's what I what I thought. Now I don't really know what to think. It's complicated."

"I can see that."

I sighed, and Carl lapsed into silence next to me.

A banging suddenly started and the cabinet under us rattled and shook. Carl and I both jumped up and backed away. The banging continued, and the muffled sounds of a woman's voice travelled through the metal.

"Someone's in there," I said.

"I know," Carl said, but neither of us made a move.

"We have to get her out," I said. Carl nodded, and finally we moved toward the cabinet. We tipped it on its side with some effort, and the voice inside groaned.

I fiddled with the door, trying to get it open, but a voice called from inside.

"No! Don't open it! I'll fry, it's Sonya."

"The sunlight," I said. "She'll burn to a crisp if we open it."

"What are we going to do?"

I thought for two seconds.

"The janitor's closet," I said. "It has no windows."

"That's downstairs," Carl said. I nodded. He sighed and braced himself at the one end of the cabinet.

I was at the other end, and we heaved and lifted it up with Sonya inside. She made small whimpering sounds as we moved her. Twice Carl dropped his end and she screamed and cursed from inside.

"Sorry," Carl muttered. He didn't have my strength.

Finally, after a lot of sweating and heaving and swearing, we finally had the cabinet in the closet between the buckets and mops and ladders. I clicked on the single light bulb that hung from the ceiling, and Carl wrestled with the now-dented door to get it open.

When he yanked it free, Sonya tumbled out. Her brown hair was disheveled and she had bruises on her face. Her hands were raw, dried blood caked around her nails, and she glared at us.

"You couldn't be a bit more careful?" she asked. Carl shrugged.

"It was either that or fried Sonya," I answered flatly. "What happened?"

Sony took a shuddering breath. "They scheduled a meeting in the middle of the night. Ruben assumed it was to talk about everything. He asked me to unlock, he'd be here literally last minute. They didn't want to talk. The moment they arrived they started trashing the place, knocking me down."

"How many were there?" I asked.

"Just the same two as last time," she said and I nodded. Carl looked at me questioningly but I would answer him later.

"Why didn't you get out of here?" I asked.

"Ruben arrived, saw them bullying me. He got them away from me into the office. One followed, the master, but the other one stuffed me in this cabinet so I couldn't go anywhere."

"It's metal," I confirmed. She hadn't been able to dematerialize.

I don't know what happened. I couldn't hear all too well through the metal and I know Ruben closed the door. The next thing there was a lot of banging around me and then the cabinet fell over."

I sat down on an upturned bucket. The closet was extremely small for the three of us and the cabinet, and I felt claustrophobic.

"He's dead, isn't he?" Sonya asked with a thin voice. I nodded. No use denying it. She covered her face with her hands and cried. Her shoulders shook and her body shrunk in on itself, crushed under the weight of her misery. Carl put a hand on her shoulder. She flinched when he did but she didn't pull away from him.

"I'm sorry," I said, and I didn't just mean for the fact that Ruben was dead. I was sorry for everything, for this happening at all, for her being involved in it, for the mess it had become.

"We have to go," Carl said. He wanted to talk, I could see it. If he was clever he would run and never look back. He would lose too much – he didn't want to be involved in this. But I knew that Carl wasn't particularly clever when it came to risking his own life. He wouldn't run. He would stay to fight. The idea should have made me feel better, that there was someone who would have my back. But it just made me feel sick to my stomach. If he died, and the chances were pretty good, his blood would be on my hands too. It would be another body to add to my growing list of losses.

"We can't open the door," I said. I looked at Sonya. She'd stopped sobbing but her cheeks were wet and her eyes were now bright and brilliant. "You'll have to get back in that thing so we can leave. You'll be able to get out again once we're gone. And then you'll have to wait it out in here until the sun goes down and you can get back home."

She didn't look happy with me but she didn't argue, either. There wasn't anything else to do about it.

She stood up and stepped back into the cabinet. Carl made sure she could push the door open from the inside before we left, so she wouldn't be stuck again, and when she was inside her little metal cabinet he opened the door and we stepped out of the closet.

"I don't know what to do with this one," Carl admitted. "We're going to have to call the police because of his death, and then they're going to go through all the paperwork. We have to get in there and remove our stuff before it comes out."

I suddenly felt like my body was made of lead. I felt heavy and sore, like I'd been the one that had been beaten up. It felt like everything that kept me going drained out of me, and I was just a shell left in the wake of destruction.

"Just call them, Carl. I'm going to go home."

"But we can't just leave—"

"It's over, Carl. Let them come. I can't do this anymore."

I turned and walked away, exiting the building. I looked up at it, and a wave of nausea and sorrow hit me. I turned my back, and drove away.

Chapter 16

The day of the attack came back to me. I'd gone to the store for my mom to buy milk. We'd been arguing about it, I'd wanted to bake sugar cookies. She'd said it wasn't necessary, there were store bought cookies in the tin and it was getting dark, too late to run out to the store for a sixteen year old. Aspen had been fourteen, stretching out her one leg on the counter and balancing on the other. She'd wanted to be a dancer. It was never too late to get fit and flexible, she'd used to say. I'd been jealous that she'd been taller than me. After that she'd never be taller than me again.

I've fought with her about my age, telling her that I was practically a grown up. Cocooned in a shell of innocence, I knew nothing. This I'd found out afterwards.

The last words I'd ever spoken to my mother was that I'd wanted her to leave me to make my own mistakes, that I didn't need her to baby me for the rest of my life.

I'd give anything to take those words back now, to tell her just one more time that I loved her, that she had made me everything I was. Well, no. Everything I used to be.

The queue at the store had been too long. Instead of turning back home I'd gone to the next one, a bit further. I'd gotten my milk but the walk home had been longer, and by the time I'd finally stepped onto the porch at the front door it had been dark. There had been no moon that night, and the world had been drenched in the inky black of night. Even the stars had looked like they'd been dimmer. I remembered it like I had photos of it, the images engraved in my mind.

I'd climbed the porch steps, and the outside light had been off. My mom usually switched it on. If I'd taken it as a sign of danger maybe things would have been different. But then again, maybe they wouldn't have. I remembered being irritated that she couldn't have left the light on for me. She'd known I'd gone out.

When I'd pushed against the front door and it swung open into a dark lounge, the smell in the air had been the first thing that caught my attention. It had smelled like fear, sour, or bitter. Something that didn't feel right. And there had been violence too. It had been my first taste of it, and it still raised like bile in my throat whenever I felt it.

I'd called out into the house, but no one had answered. I'd walked through the lounge and into the dining room.

The table had been overturned. Chairs lay scattered across the floor, some splintered. The vase that had been in the center of the table had been shattered and lay in shards on the ground. The water had made a wet patch around the shattered glass and flowers that lay in a chaotic heap, like whatever had happened at caused it to wet its pants.

I'd reached for the light switch automatically, even though a voice in my head had kept screaming that I should have turned and run. But my hand had reached out and flipped the switch. The white light had been blinding at first. And then it had shown me the ugly truth.

There had been blood on the carpets. The metallic smell of it pinched my nose, and I gagged, covering my nose with my hand. The milk I'd been carrying fell to the ground, the contained split open and the white liquid spread in a point across the carpet.

I'd followed the trail of the stain, and under the table, that I had only noticed then was broken, was a body. My mother's body. Her short blond hair had been tousled and fanned out around her head like a halo. Her arm had been bent at an impossible angle, and when I took two steps closer I'd seen what I'd already known. Her face had been covered in blood, the soft hazel color of her eyes had stared vacantly at the chaos around her. Her throat had been ripped on the side, bloody.

I'd covered my mouth and screamed into my hand. My whole body had started trembling and I'd felt like the life had been draining out of me.

A crash in the next room had pulled me out of my state of shock, and I'd whirled around. Aspen and my dad, if whoever had done this were still there I had to stop them before I lost more people I loved.

I'd run to Aspen's bedroom where the crash had come from. I'd kicked the door open and it had bounced back, nearly hitting me in the face, but what I'd seen had been enough to shoulder the blow. Aspen had laid the floor, her body twisted and bent just above the hips, where it hadn't been supposed to do that. Her eyes had been closed and for two seconds I'd feared the worst, but then she'd whimpered, the tiniest sign, but a shred of hope I'd been able to cling on to.

"Where are they?" I asked her in a loud whisper, hoping she'd respond, but she'd only whimpered again, her head lolling to the side. Her light skin had been an ash-grey and there'd been blood on her clothes. I'd ripped the material aside and noticed the blood hadn't been hers.

A sound behind me had made me spin around, and my dad had stood there, his fangs bare. He'd had blood smeared across his face and chest, and he'd hissed at me.

"Dad?" I'd asked in a small voice, and then I'd noticed the fire poker he'd held in his hands. It had blood on it, the tip dripping red. My mom's image had flashed in front of my eyes again, and I'd lost it.

I was only half-vampire, but in a situation of life and death the animal in me came out just like with any pure pred. I'd hissed back at my dad even though I had no sharp needle teeth to show. He'd swung that poker at me and struck me in the neck. It had burned, and I could feel the blood pouring out of the gash, hot liquid oozing down my neck and staining my shirt.

I hadn't wasted time. I'd jumped on him, ducking underneath the poker he'd lifted to swing against, and tackled him through the open door and against the opposite passage wall. The knock had winded us both, but I'd been beyond the point of no return. In my rage I'd seen a white light, my dead mother, and my broken sister. And in front of me had been the man responsible.

Anger made anyone stronger. I was a testimony to that. The police had finally pulled me off my dad, who's face had been purple, flowering with bruises and blood where I'd hit him way past unconsciousness with my bare hands.

My mother had been pronounced dead on the scene. My sister had been taken to a hospital. I'd been booked into therapy.

Years of therapy did nothing. All the therapist did for me was remind me of that awful day over and over again. And I'd hated every minute of it, until I had been eighteen and old enough to tell my foster parents I wasn't going anymore. Aspen had been in a wheelchair after being hospitalized for a month, and no amount of therapy would have been able to erase what had happened to her.

I'd stayed out of the way of vampires since then. I'd avoided the dark, slept with a nightlight like a child, and I'd be in before sunset every evening. One night it had rained so hard I'd been stranded at the gym in college. Howling winds had ripped through the trees and no one dared go out. By the time the storm had subsided it had been dark and I'd been terrified.

I'd walked the quiet streets home, keeping my ears open, suppressing the fear of the dark that I'd been kindling for over two years. A vampire had appeared next to me, a man that had a nasty cut across his face which reminded me too much of the scar that had formed in my neck. He'd grinned at me and his vampire teeth, although yellow, had brought back the flash of my bloodstained father, attacking me.

I'd attacked the vampire before he'd been able to think twice, and I'd killed him. When I'd stood in the alley, blood on my hands and my heart beating in my throat, a voice had rung out to me.

"You have skills," he'd said. I'd swung around and backed away, scared he'd call the police.

"You hate vampires," he'd said again, a statement, not a question. "I know someone that I'd like you to meet."

He'd pulled out a card with Ruben's firm name and number on it.

"This is an accounting firm," I'd said, confused.

"Just call him. Tell him Carl sent you. He'll know."

He'd turned and sauntered down the street without a care in the world.

"Why?" I'd called after him.

"You have rage, kid. In this life, we can use that kind of thing."

After that he'd disappeared.

Working for Ruben had been quick and painless. I'd spent one night out with Carl, and for a week I'd had nightmares after I'd seen him work. I'd gone back after that, and told Ruben I wanted to do it permanently. He'd told me everything I already knew, that I'd need to train, that it wasn't going to be easy, that it would border on illegal activities. But I'd agreed because it meant I could kill vampires. I hadn't been able to kill my dad. Maybe if they hadn't come in time to save him I would have. But there were so many other mundane vampires around since the laws let them roam free, and it hadn't been long before Carl had started avoiding me because I'd been better, because the rookie was outshining him and jealousy didn't look good on a man with his physique.

I'd taken the job because somehow it had felt like every vampire I killed was one less in the world that could get to Aspen. In a wheelchair she was vulnerable, and I couldn't run the risk of another monster suddenly going rogue.

The fact that there never really was a chance for that anymore was something I ignored.

And after all that, after training for years and killing vampires every week night the way other people went in to the office, I'd managed to fail her again.

I sat on my bike after I'd parked in front of my apartment and took a deep breath. I closed my eyes and focused on the blood that surged through my veins. I could still feel her, a feint pulse next to my own. She was still alive.

Every time I checked in to find out I held my breath, hoping for the best but preparing myself for the worst. And every time I found she was still alive, I felt relief so strongly I felt like I might crumble.

But still I couldn't pin a location. It was like someone knew that this was what had happened, that I had my own tracker on her, and they stopped me from finding her. It was like a metal wall between us, and try as I might, I couldn't get through it.

I pushed the bike into my crumby garage and rolled the door shut with a terrible noise. I clicked the lock shut and made my way into the building. Everything in my apartment was as I'd left it before, and I felt safe enough to take my guns off and put them away. I still had my Glock under my pillow and I kept the knife on me in the thigh sheath just in case.

I sat down at the booth in the kitchen and stared at the empty seat opposite me. How long had it been – a week? – since Jennifer had sat across from me? It had looked like such an innocent job then. Distasteful, but innocent. It was difficult to think things had gotten so bent out of shape in such a short time.

I'd lost Joel, the only friend I ever had. And I knew it was my fault. They'd taken him either as a warning, or as bait. They might have killed him. I didn't know. And I had no way to know if he was still alive the way I was tracing signs of life from Aspen. He could be dead for all I knew, and I knew it was all my fault.

A dark cloud formed above me, and it colored my mood black.

Ruben was dead. That was my fault too, because I hadn't done my job. If only I'd understood how serious it was, if only I'd taken him more seriously and done what he'd asked. But his cocky attitude and the arrogance with which he talked about the night world when he knew nothing about it annoyed me, and I showed that to him by lack of respect.

Now he was dead, and there was nothing I could do about it. And Sonya? It was dumb luck that she was still alive, and no one knew what would happen to her now. Maybe they would come after her too, in case she knew something. In that case that would be another mark on my name. Another life to feel guilty about.

I folded my arms on the table top and rested my head on them. My breath bounced off the plastic and came back into my face, making a warm little furnace that painted my face with my own breath.

I sighed. The only way I was going to get any further was to get to the bottom of the master vampires and how they operated. If I knew what they did, what skills they possessed and how they did their business, I could find out more. I could find some kind of crack in their metal wall and find Aspen.

The only person that knew anything about the masters, was Connor. I was damn glad I'd missed when I'd shot him. I needed him alive now to tell me.

At the same time I knew that it was ridiculous even trying to go to him after that. He would never help me, why would he? And after what happened between us, after the night we'd spent together... I pushed the memories away. They made my throat swell shut and I didn't know if it was because I hated the memories, or because it hurt that Connor probably didn't want me anymore. I didn't want to find out, either.

I had to find him if I wanted to find Aspen, no matter how horrible it was going to be. So that was what I was going to do. And the only person I could rely on for that right now was Jennifer.

There were so many obstacles in front of me now I didn't feel like dealing with, but I didn't have a choice.

I found her card in the drawer I'd dumped it in after I'd visited her the last time. There were a couple of people on my list of least-favorite characters in the world. She'd made it on. I didn't appreciate liars. I had a hell of a life I covered up all the time but I avoided lying if I could. The only thing left in the world that people had, even when everything else was stripped away and they had nothing, was their word. And if your word was good for nothing, you had nothing left.

The phone rang seven times. One more time and it would roll over to voice mail. But it didn't. She answered.

"I need to see you," I said into the phone. She hesitated for a moment.

"I don't know if that's a good idea."

"Why not? Don't you think that you owe me, at least?" I knew it wasn't the best card to play, but I was running out of options with Aspen and I needed Jennifer to play along. At least for one more night.

"Look, you're not the kind of person I should be having contact with right now. If they hear that I've spoken to you, after everything..."

"The master vampires? Have they contacted you?"

If they'd threatened Jennifer but she was still alive, she had something on them. And if she refused to speak to me, there was nothing I could do. I was getting desperate.

"I just need to find—"

"Don't say it," Jennifer cut me off. "Don't. I can't do this."

She hung up on me. The line beeped in my ear and I swore, throwing my phone onto the bed. Dammit.

Two seconds later it beeped. It was a message from Jennifer.

They're watching me. I didn't want to talk on the phone. Meet me at Fiasco at nine.

It was still a while before dark, but at least now I had something to do again once the sun was down. Without a job I felt untethered, and I didn't want to think what sitting at home twiddling my thumbs would be like.

I showered and got dressed. I put on my leathers again. I wasn't going out for kills just yet, but I didn't know what information would come to light, and if I was going to get Aspen out of there later, I wanted to be ready.

I loaded my guns. Silver bullets in each of them. I had my Smith & Wesson on me, my SIG at my back and my knife on my thigh. I had an ankle holster where I secured my Glock, and I put the Carbine in my bike's compartment. I didn't want to be caught off guard and if I wanted to get Aspen out of there alive, me too, for that matter, I had to go in there guns blazing.

My phone rang on the bed where I left it.

"What is it?" I asked into the speaker. I was in a foul mood, pumped full of adrenaline in anticipation for the night, and in a foul mood because I had to wait.

"Don't sound so happy to hear from me," Carl's sarcasm came through the phone.

"What do you want, Carl?"

"I told you, I want in. I want to know where you're headed later. You can do with some back up once in a while."

I shook my head even though Carl couldn't see it. "I'm not going out to kill. I need to contact some people first, and you're not coming with me."

"Don't cut me out of this now, Adele. I want to avenge Ruben just as much as you do."

I hadn't thought about it. I didn't want avenge Ruben. His death was tragic, and the guilt for it would chew away at me for a very, very long time. But I wasn't out to avenge his death and make it right. I was going to get Aspen. I wondered what Ruben and Carl had going that *he* felt the need to avenge him.

"Look, I'm just going to talk to someone. If I know more, I'll call you, okay?"

Carl mumbled something that sounded unhappy, but he agreed. I hung up the phone and closed my eyes, taking a deep breath. It didn't matter how badly he wanted to get in on this. I wasn't going to drag him along. Carl was just a human, and even though I hated his guts most of the time I wasn't going to drag him into a situation where he could get killed, too. There was enough blood on my hands already.

It was finally time to leave and I pulled out, my bike growling into the night. It sounded the way I felt. I made it through town, weaving in and out of traffic, and I parked in front of Fiasco. When I stepped onto the deck where the outside tables were arranged, I noticed Jennifer sitting in the back looking like she was trying to make herself small and invisible.

"You're not really fooling anyone trying to hide like that," I said. "You're not invisible."

I sat down and a waiter appeared immediately.

"Water," I said. I didn't like anything else, and alcohol was off limits for me. It made me buzz and I couldn't go out on a killing spree on that level. It would be asking for trouble.

Jennifer rolled her eyes.

"What do you want?" she asked me. Her voice was calm but her eyes kept darting around the place, looking for faces.

"Who are you hiding from?" I asked.

"I can't really be seen with you. I've been warned."

"By them?" I didn't have to clarify who I meant by 'them'. Jennifer nodded.

"They called me yesterday and told me that if I talk to you, I'm dead."

For someone who was walking around with a death sentence, she was damn brave to be our here talking to me. The water arrived and we both kept quiet while the waitress put the cold glass in front of me. When she was walked away I took a sip and kept quiet until I was sure everyone was out of earshot.

"What do you have on them?" I asked. She frowned at me.

"They have to have a reason why you're still alive. They already killed a handful of people to get what they want."

Jennifer's face blanched. "They have?"

I nodded. I wasn't going to go into it. I didn't want to tell everyone how much I messed up. And I didn't want to think about it too much myself, either.

"So?" I prodded.

Jennifer took a shaky breath and looked down at her hands. She was fiddling with a napkin, tearing it into tiny pieces, making a pile on the table. "It's not really something I have on them. It's more like it's just something they need. They can't kill me as long as they need the funding for their... business. Connor's account has my name in there, too. I'm allowed to say what happens to the money, and as long as I'm alive they have the money. They can't kill me, it's one they can't crack. Unless they can find funding somewhere else."

I was horrified. Jennifer was letting this carry on.

"Why don't you cut off funding?" I asked. "You're just letting this continue and you know it's wrong."

When Jennifer looked up at me her eyes were rimmed with tears. Again. She was really quick to cry.

"If I do, they'll kill me. This is the only thing that's keeping me alive. With what I know... they'll kill me. It's the lesser of two evils."

Something inside me closed. I wasn't going to fall for that one. The lesser of two evils was what I'd chosen. To keep my sister alive no matter what. But if it came down to the greater good I'd sacrifice myself. The only reason I couldn't do it now was because I was the only person left to care for her, the only person that could bring her back.

"You're disgusting," I said and I meant it. Judging by the look of shame on her face, something mixed with anger, I could tell she knew it, too.

"What did you want from me?" she asked in a cold voice.

Right. The reason I came. I needed information from her, and I just told her how appalling I thought she was. Great.

"I need to find Connor," I said.

Jennifer shook her head.

"Why would I know where he is? Since he disappeared..." She swallowed hard and looked down at her pile of napkin shreds. "He's dead to me now. He's cut himself off from everyone, I don't know where he is."

I'd expected her to answer that. But I wasn't going to give up.

"Give me an address. Something. Anything, Jennifer. Otherwise a lot more people will die. I need to stop this."

I don't know if it was something in my face or my voice, or because she felt condemned, but she nodded and pulled out a notepad and pen. She scribbled on it and slid it across the table.

It had two addresses on it. The mansion in Caldwell Street in Westham Hills. That had belonged to him after all. And the address of his offices. The Palace.

"If you want to go to the offices, just use my name and they should let you in. The night guards know me."

I bet they did. I thanked her and got up, my glass of water hardly touched. At least I hadn't ordered something that had cost money. I walked to my bike and got on. It was nine thirty. I'd only spoken to Jennifer for half an hour. My phone rang just as I was about to pull off.

"You owe me money," Carlos said.

"I know. I'll bring it to you—"

"Now. I don't like waiting. I can't afford to give my clients credit."

His voice was hard. I guessed this was as tough as his life got. I sighed and pulled the phone away from my ear for a second to check the time.

"I'll drop by later tonight," I said. "I have errands to run."

"You can't—"I hung up. I didn't feel like arguing about it. Yes, I hadn't paid him and I was in the wrong. But that was how it was and I would fix it once I had the chance.

Chapter 17

The roads were quieting down, most people settling down into their weeknight routines. I was the only one that was out of mine. If it had been an ordinary life, I would have been heading out from the office with a stack of papers from Ruben and a night of blood and guts before me.

I wanted to go back to that. It hadn't been a hell of a job, and there'd always been a little torn. But it had been familiar. Safe, ironically. It had been my life.

What did I have now? A big mess to clear up before it was all too late.

The neighborhood felt like it always did, with so many suburban families home. The neighborhood buzzed with vibrant life, if not happiness then at least contentment. Families were together, I could feel the strength of their bonds as I passed the houses. It made me feel strangely untethered, like an island. Surrounded by nothing but ocean. Disconnected from everything else like me.

I cut the engine before I got to Connor's house and rolled the last couple of feet. He had probably heard me coming, who was I fooling? He was a pure bred, with hearing that out-matched my own. But it made me feel better to do it this way. It made me feel like somehow I still had control.

I parked my bike and slid off it, walking up the dark drive way. I was aware again of the strong scent of night flowers. The jasmine hung the thickest in the air, and I couldn't decide if I liked it or hated it. Smells had so many memories, good and bad. I tried the front door, the only entrance to the house I hadn't actually used before, and found it unlocked. It was a surprise. If Connor was home I expected him to have stronger security.

Clyde, the mean old house cat, came to the door with a low moaning sound that warned me off.

"Get over it," I sneered at the cat. I was irritated tonight that it didn't like me sometimes. I was irritated in general, tonight, and I was taking it out on a stupid cat.

I worked from the one room to the next, systematically checking it. I had my SIG out, gripped in two hands and pointed toward the floor. I didn't want to shoot Connor, for once, but I didn't want to run into unwanted company either. After all, the door had been unlocked.

When I got to the office, a room I'd only been in once before, Connor stood in it with his back to me.

"So, you've decided to have another run at it," he said, not looking at me. His voice was dull, empty. He sounded bored. But the muscles in his back were tense, both his feet were planted firmly on the ground, and I knew all his attention was on me, not on the papers he was flipping through.

"I'm not here to kill you," I said. My voice sounded thin, nothing like the person I usually was. And I didn't feel big and tough, either. I had three guns on me, and I'd never been so nervous in my life.

I tucked my SIG back into my waistband to prove my point. Connor wasn't looking at me, but I didn't doubt that he heard.

"I know you're not," he said. Finally he turned to me. His face seemed paler than it was before, his eyes had faint circles underneath them. He looked taller, and the skin on his face clung to the bone so I could see the structure of his skull. I wanted to ask for a moment if he was alright, but it wasn't my place.

"I need your help," I said. It wasn't in my nature to ask for help, to grovel, but everyone had their breaking points.

"What for?" I'd expected an immediate no. His answer sparked a little hope inside of me.

"I need to find the masters. I need know how to find them. They're angry, and at some point I'm going to have to face them."

"Well, that can't be chalked up to failure on your part," he said, his voice cold and hard. "After all, you did shoot me. I was just lucky enough that I was faster than that bullet."

"Connor..." What could I say? 'Sorry' didn't exactly cut it. 'Oh, my bad, I know I shot you but hey we can put it behind us, right?' Sure.

"I'd like for you to leave," he said and walked past me.

"Connor, please. I... they have Aspen."

I hated to admit my weakness. I hated that I was begging for help. But there was nothing I wouldn't do for my sister. And if I had to give the upper hand to my mark, well, I would do that.

"At this point, Adele, I don't really think I want to help you. I've done more than enough to try and show you that you're above all this. That you're worth more."

And all this time I'd thought he'd intentionally been driving me crazy. A sharp pain shot into my chest.

"I fell for you," he admitted. "God knows that was the biggest mistake in the world. Who falls for the girl that's trying to kill you?"

"Why did you?" I asked because suddenly I was dying to know what anyone could see in me other than a monster. That's all that I saw in the mirror anymore. I had that horrible scar and eyes that promised nothing but death, and I dressed it all up in leathers and guns that drove the point home. Literally and figuratively.

"How can someone like you think anything... good... about me?"

He chuckled without expression on his face. "I don't even know the answer to that," he said and his words stung. "You see, there was a time when I believed that I could see the beauty in you, despite all the ugliness you're trying to bury it with. I wanted to believe that I could change you, that I could show you what it was like to have something to live for again. Something that would stop you looking over your shoulder, back at your father."

I suddenly felt like there wasn't a single bone in my body. I reached out for the wall to steady myself before I lost my balance.

"How did you know?" I asked, my voice brittle.

"Your secrets may not be in the news now, Adele, but they were once upon a time. It didn't take a lot of digging to get the story. Not that I can even begin to imagine what you're dealing with, but I told myself that what you were doing was justifiable."

"And still you think I'm the monster," I sneered. I was getting closer and closer to crying, and I had to make a plan to make the tears go away, fast. Being mean was the only way I knew how, even if it meant it hurt me more.

"I don't think you're a monster. At least, I didn't. But it takes a lot for someone to shoot the man she's just slept with point blank. I'm not so sure anymore."

I took a deep breath and it was shaky. It made me sound weak. I looked weak, and I knew it. And I hated it.

"Please just help me with Aspen," I said. "Then you can hate me forever."

Connor smiled but it didn't reach his eyes.

"I'm sorry, princess," he said, and then he disappeared. I was left alone in the empty house. Clyde padded into the room silently, and mewed.

"Shut up," I said and left the house.

My eyes burned and I tore full throttle down the road. Everything around me faded to a blur and the wind whipped around me, yanking at my emotions. I prayed they would blow away with the speed.

I made it to the ugly side of town in under five minutes and I was sure there were about six cameras with my plates on it now. But I didn't care. Joel could squash them for me again.

Joel.

My stomach contracted and I felt like I was going to throw up. If he was dead... I didn't even want to think about it. I was becoming more and more aware that I was completely alone. I had no one left. I wasn't one of those people who knew a million people with a huge social life. But I did have people, and the ones that I had I held dear.

And one by one they were being ripped away from me. That was why I was in this filthy neighborhood, where the garbage lay in the streets like a twisted insight to the type of people that lived here. The night was quiet, and there wasn't a light on in any of the windows I passed. Not even the street lights were on despite the fact that it was going on to eleven.

I parked in front of the rundown building where Carlos lived. At night it was even worse, the whole place seemed to have sunken in on itself. When I stepped into the lobby it really did feel haunted. Everything was dark, the counter where the doorman should have been a black gaping hole. I hurried through it and towards the passage where I would find Carlos's door.

When I reached it I stretched out my hand to knock, but I caught myself. The door wasn't closed completely. It was slightly ajar. Inside was quiet, no music blaring through like the last time I'd been here.

"Please, no," I whispered. If Carlos was dead it would be all my fault.

"Well, we didn't expect to see you here," a voice purred around me. I couldn't tell where it was coming from, and I recognized the echoing quality and the soft, seductive tone. I spun around. She laughed and it danced around me like chimes in the wind.

Creepy chimes in a horror movie.

"You're just a surprise every time, aren't you?" she spoke again. Her words echoed in a whisper after the spoken sentence had fallen quiet, and my skin crawled. I looked up and down the passage, relying on my other senses because I couldn't see in the dark, but it was difficult to tell where she was. She was very good at making it sound like she was everywhere at once. If I lived through this I really had to write a book on her kind so that the next vampire slayer wouldn't get beaten up the way I constantly did.

"What's wrong, Celia?" I asked, using her name for the first time. "Too scared to come out and face me? Is that why you're hiding?"

She laughed again, and it was laced with malice. I knew she wasn't scared. There was arrogance in the air, and confidence. If there was fear, it was mine. But I needed her to come out and show herself, because as much as I hated to admit it, I couldn't find her.

I stepped back into the lobby. The place gave me the creeps. Celia laughed again, and this time it came from one place. The dark area where the counter was. Well, that made sense.

When I took a step closer, I saw her. Only a dark shape, crouching on the counter, but her eyes glowed green, giving her away. I reached behind my back to pull my gun, but she launched for me and she was quicker than I was. She managed to knock me to the ground even with my attempt to duck. I hit the ground and for a moment I couldn't breathe. I lifted up my arms and gasped for breath.

"You shouldn't challenge me if you're not ready to face me," Celia said, and her voice was sweet and sultry.

"Oh, I'm ready," I said, pushing myself up. I was more than fed up with this woman. I'd taken out my gun, the S&W and I held it tight, my fingers curling around the butt of it like it was a lifeline. She was quick, but if I could get this one fired at her, she wouldn't live to laugh about it. I took aim at her, the dark shadow with the gleaming eyes, and pulled the trigger.

A shot rang and the plaster splintered. A big gash in the wooden wall showed me where the bullet had hit. And she laughed again. Dammit.

"Don't bring a sword to a gun fight," she chanted, and her words danced around me.

"Isn't it the other way round?" I asked. I was the one with the gun.

"Well, yes. But it doesn't matter, really."

She kicked me on the jaw out of nowhere and I saw stars. The gun fell and bounced away, I heard the dull thud in the darkness. As long as she didn't find it, I would be alright. The world tilted and my head hit the floor. I lay on the ground, trying to find my bearings. The carpet was rough and gritty under my cheek. When I tried to get up, my head spun and I felt nauseous. That was going to be a concussion.

She waited for me to pull myself together and get back up before she struck again. I was ready for her this time, and I got in a blow. I imagined I'd given her a bloody nose, at least, but I wasn't sure. I unsheathed the knife at my thigh, and held the blade away from me. A shadow moved in the corner of my eye and I slashed without thinking.

I cut something. She screamed with an unearthly howl and my blade had blood on it. Where I got her, I didn't know.

"You have to stop doing that," she sneered. I knew she was hurting. I could hear it in her voice. There were very few supernatural creatures that could withstand silver. I had a mild reaction to it, like an allergy, but I had it the easiest because I was a half breed with vampire blood. I didn't have the ability to change into a monster like most were creatures – which included her – so silver wasn't that big a deal.

I reached behind my back for my SIG. I wanted to kill the bitch.

Her next attack was slower, and I knew I'd cut her somewhere it mattered, but she was faster than my gun and she got it out of my hand too. She still put up a damn good fight, and she came in with claws, ready to scratch my eyes out.

I was just as eager to get to hers. I punched her in the face. She managed to scratch me down the throat but I already had a scar there and it wasn't going to slow me down. I managed to elbow her in the gut and she doubled over, gasping for breath. I jammed my knee up to hit her in the face but she'd already recovered and straightened out. She knocked me, hard, and I lost my grip on the knife. It clattered into the dark. I still had the Glock on me, but she wasn't giving me time to draw it. She snatched out her arm faster than I'd ever seen before, and grabbed my hair, yanking it. Hard.

I pain shot into my head and I bent over backwards, the force pushing me off balance. I fell to the floor. She didn't let up. She kicked me while I was down, in the ribs, in the stomach, two kicks to the head. I couldn't think about moving anymore. I curled into a ball, and let it rain on me. There was nothing else to do but hope I survived.

After what felt like forever it finally stopped. I lay there, curled in a ball, for a long time. I guessed she was gone, but I didn't know. I was struggling to think. Every bone in my body ached, and I knew from experience I would have more than a couple of bruises. I was sure I was bleeding somewhere, too. I could feel it drain out of me, taking my energy, my strength, along with it.

I heard footsteps. I didn't have the energy for more. So I closed my eyes and let the darkness surround me. If it called me home, I would go.

I woke up in a blue room. The covers over me were heavy, and when I moved to get them off me I groaned. Everything hurt. It felt like I'd been dragged for miles. I couldn't open my one eye all the way, I figured it would be black then, too. I did a quick inventory. Nothing broken. I could deal with that.

"You're up," someone said at the door, and when I looked Carlos stood there, leaning against the door post with his arms crossed over his chest.

"What time is it?" I asked. Carlos frowned but looked at his wristwatch.

"Eight," he said.

"Tuesday?" I asked. My worst fear was having lost days. I couldn't afford that. But Carlos nodded.

"You took quite a beating," he said.

"She was here," I answered and swallowed. Talking hurt.

"I tried to tell you not to come. The masters were checking me out."

"Am I going to get you in trouble?" I asked. I didn't know if I had what it took to have more blame shifted onto me.

"I think it will be okay. I'm pretty sure they think you're dead. *I* thought you were dead when I found you."

I pushed myself up and groaned.

"You really shouldn't be up," he said. "You can stay at least until you can move."

"I can move," I said and it took everything for me to get myself out of the bed. "I have a training session at nine."

"I don't think that's wise," he said.

"And yet, you're working for vampires and I'm killing people." He shut up because it was true. Neither of us was very clever if that was what we'd chosen to do with our lives.

"I owe you money," I said.

Carlos shook his head. "Don't worry about it. You got assaulted in my building. I think we can wait with that."

I nodded and regretted it. My head thumped painfully. I tried to stretch myself out. Everything ached. My ribs were badly bruised, I could feel it when I moved, and there was something wrong with my wrist. I couldn't move my hand without it hurting.

"Maybe I'll take it slow on the hand-to-hand combat today," I said to Carlos. He just shook his head.

It took me a full hour to make my way to the Academy. Sensei was waiting for me. When he saw me he pulled up his eyebrows.

He walked to me and put his hands on my shoulders, looking at me with a lot of worry on his face. I was pretty sure I looked like hell. I could feel it.

"Want to tell me what's going on?" he asked.

I lowered myself to the ground, slipping out from underneath his hands, and managed to lie down. He stood over me like a towering sentry. I winced, moving around until I lay down on my back and nothing hurt when I didn't move.

"Not really," I answered.

"Let me rephrase. Tell me what's going on." He sat down next to me, watching, and he wouldn't take no for an answer.

I closed my eyes and took a deep breath. And then I told him. I told him about my job. I told him about Jennifer and her strange request, and my ridiculous act of kindness where I saved the vampire I should just have killed in the first place. I told him about Ruben, the man who had been so arrogant I couldn't stand him, and now that he was gone he was the guy I missed. The masters of the city, Celia, Connor.

Aspen and Joel were lost to me, I was sure of it, and I might have dragged more people into it by going to Carlos, and promising Carl he could have a hand in what was going on. I didn't even want to think of Sonya.

When I finished, there was a moment of silence. Sensei just looked at me, and I wondered if he hated me now.

"You've been training to fight supernatural creatures all this time?" he asked. I nodded as well as I could managed, which wasn't very well at all.

"Why didn't you tell me?"

"Would you have believed me?"

He was silent, thinking about it. I expected a no.

"I would have trained you differently," he finally said. "I don't think you should train today though."

I chuckled and a sharp pain shot into my chest. I groaned. "I didn't really come here to train."

"Then why did you come?"

I sighed, a lump rising in my throat out of nowhere. "You're all I have left." My voice as thick and my throat felt tight, like I was having an allergic reaction. Yeah, allergic. To emotions. That's what I was. "Aspen and Joel might as well be dead by now. I don't even know anymore. I've lost Ruben and Zelda, and I wouldn't be surprised if Sonya and Carlos turn up dead too. I just can't..." I took a deep breath and blew it out with again. "I just can't save everyone."

I blinked furiously, trying to get the tears that were stinging my eyes to go away.

"Can I ask you a question?" Sensei's voice was soft and calm, and when I turned my head to look at him he wasn't staring at me with dagger eyes or closed off and resigned from me forever. In fact, I couldn't read any kind of emotion at all.

"What?" I asked.

"Why do you do it?"

"Kill vampires?"

He nodded.

"Because I have to make sure she's safe. My father... I can't do it all again."

Sensei was quiet again. I'd only touched on the topic of my father. There was no way I was going to be able to talk about that in detail without having a full scale meltdown. Not now.

"You need help," he finally said.

"Yeah, thanks for that," I snapped. I took a deep breath and forced myself to calm down. It was hard to be angry and aggressive with so many injuries. "You're probably right though."

He chuckled. "I didn't mean professionally, although I don't think you've been handling it quite the way you should have... but I meant that you need people that back you up so you can end this."

"What do you mean?"

"I mean you have friends that are willing to help you. So let them."

I pushed myself up and wiped my good eye with the back of my hand.

"I can't let more people sacrifice their lives for me. I've lost too many already."

"Have you asked them?" he asked. "Maybe they want to do this for you."

I shook my head, and Sensei got up and stood in front of me. He looked tall, from where I sat on the floor.

"I know I would," he said, and smiled.

"Why?" I asked.

"Some things are worth fighting for."

It was the second time in two days that someone had mentioned my worth. It was a difficult pill to swallow. Since the accident I'd figured myself to be worthless. It was easy to flirt with death when you were disposable.

"Come on," Sensei said and held out his hand to help me up.

"Where are we going?"

"You need real medication."

Chapter 18

By the time I had painkillers in my system I started to feel like I wasn't on the brink of death anymore. My eye was still swollen and the lopsided vision annoyed me, but my head didn't throb so much and the hopeless pool of despair I'd been set on drowning myself in had somehow drained.

It still hurt to move, something horrible ached in my ribs, almost like they were broken, but I knew out of experience that that was much worse.

When Sensei was done with me, he offered me coffee.

I hadn't had something as simple as coffee in a while, and when he handed me the cup the warmth travelled into my hands and up my arms. It was nice. When last had I focused on something that was just nice?

"What do I do now?" I asked.

I knew I wanted to go get Aspen. I could tell she was still alive. Half of me didn't feel like it had died yet and if I focused very hard I could still find her pulse, although my headache, still faintly there, made it harder.

I wanted to go get her, and get Joel. Now that my moment of self-pity was over and I felt like I could carry on again, a terrible anger bubbled up inside of me. The kind of anger that could roll over into rage if I wasn't careful. The kind of anger that had me attack my father when he hurt my sister.

"Now you decide if it really was worth being a one woman act all this time," Sensei said. I closed my eyes and took a deep breath. Asking for help wasn't a strong suit. In fact, it made me feel weak, having to rely on someone else. Besides that I wasn't good at trusting someone else, so this was really a tough one.

"Everyone that's gotten involved so far got killed, and that was without me asking them." I could still place some – definitely not all, not even most – of the blame on them for getting involved because it was what they had wanted. Ruben had taken on a job that had been too much for him. My fault because I'd messed around. His fault because he'd been stupid. Joel had known what hacking could do. He'd had the warnings. My fault because he would do anything for me without asking. His fault because he knew what his line of work could hold for him. Zelda had been my fault. She'd protected Aspen when I couldn't. Aspen had been my fault because I'd taken a job I'd been arrogant enough to think was easy.

I was starting to realize that the arrogance and pride I'd been building for a while had been ridiculous. I'd been playing in a tide pool when the ocean out there was much bigger. And I'd crowned myself queen thinking I was winning.

The truth was I hadn't been winning at all. I'd been losing. The only person I'd been fooling was myself. The real facts were that Ruben was using me as an assassin for lower class problems that no one tried to sort out differently. I was a murderer, hiding in the dark, nothing more. I'd thought I was bigger than my problems by choosing to take jobs that were smaller than me. I was an illusionist.

The job that had been too big for me, too big for Ruben, had been a coincidence. I was starting to realize I couldn't beat Celia, not because she was too good, but just because I'd never really been good enough.

And now I wanted to take on master vampires because of a mess I'd created in my ignorance. And I had no idea how we would make it out alive.

"What if we all die?" I asked. Sensei shrugged.

"None of us will be around to remember it, in that case."

I chuckled without much emotion. Blunt honesty. He knew how to hand me the truth.

I took another deep breath.

"Sensei, will you help me?"

He looked at me and smiled.

"Sure," he said, like I'd asked if I could borrow a book.

"You may die," I pointed out, suddenly feeling like I'd made a mistake. He looked way too happy to be involved in this. Maybe he didn't understand.

He shrugged again.

"Maybe this isn't a good idea," I said, shaking my head as slowly as I much as I would dare. I liked him. He was a great guy, a good teacher, and the only ray of hope this horrible mess had offered. I didn't want to be the reason for his death.

"I'll help," he said. "You asked. It's all I've been waiting for."

He had hinted at it a couple of times. I sighed and he rubbed his hands together like he was going to get something nice out of it.

"Call me Phil," he said.

Phil? I'd never known his name. To me he'd always just been Sensei.

"Phil..." I said, trying it on for size. It seemed strange to call him by his first name. It made us seem... equal.

"Right. Now. Who else can you call?"

I thought for a moment, then pulled out my phone. Carl answered on the second ring.

"Can you meet me?" I asked. I gave him an address and he hung up, promising he would be here. I wondered if the man ever slept. I never seemed to catch him in his downtime.

He arrived at the Martial Arts Academy in less than twenty minutes. When he walked in Sensei – Phil, I should say – and Carl sized each other up like boxers in a ring.

"Carl," he introduced himself tightly.

"Phil," the response came. The atmosphere was tense as they looked each other over. But then it eased, and they shook hands.

Whatever had happened had been smoothed over by them without any words. They had decided they liked each other.

"So, what's up?" he asked me.

"You said you wanted in on the action."

He nodded.

"Well, in a nutshell, my sister and technician have been taken by master vampires that are a hell of a lot stronger than the ones we've been pretending to be boss over. They also have a deadly cat woman as a pet that doesn't stand down. I want to go get them."

"Do you know where they are?" he asked.

"No idea."

He nodded, looking thoughtful.

"Do you know how to defeat master vampires and the cat lady?"

I shook my head, admitting failure. Carl looked like he was still thinking, and to be honest I expected him to say no. I wanted him to say no. I wanted him to go home where he could be the asshole I didn't like, because I preferred asshole Carl to dead Carl. But he shrugged in much the same way Sensei, Phil, had responded, like it was no big deal.

"Sure," he said.

I shook my head. Two men in front of me willing to sacrifice their lives when they knew it meant almost certain death. And here I'd been thinking I was crazy. I was feeling more and more optimistic that being perpetually angry was a small problem compared to raving lunatic.

"So, what's the plan?" Carl asked.

I hesitated. I hadn't really thought that far. When he looked at me he barked a laugh.

"Two humans and a half-breed? I don't know. You're good, Adele, but I think we need something else."

He was right. As offensive as he was, it was the truth, and if we wanted anything to happen, we needed something else.

Someone else.

"I have to go," I said. "I'll meet you guys back here in an hour."

"Are you going to get someone?" Carl asked.

"I don't know." I had no idea what would happen. "But when I come back, if I came back, it will either be me, or I'll have someone with me."

They both just nodded. I turned to leave, but not before I noticed the look Phil and Carl were giving each other. It wasn't very friendly. I didn't have time or energy to worry about them. I got on my bike and pulled out. Just maneuvering the machine that was technically too big for me took more effort than I would have liked. How was I going to fight if I had this many injuries? Hopefully my vampire blood would do its magic and heal me up quicker.

I wanted to shake my head but instead I just mentally shook off the worries that wouldn't do for now. I didn't want to let my headache come back. It had slipped back into a dull thud at the back of my head, much better than the sharp pain that had been like a thousand chisels in my temples.

I was daylight and I didn't expect I would get anywhere. But I had to try, one last time. There was only one person that I knew that knew the masters well enough to help me. Jennifer knew them, but she was just a human, and it took a vampire to know a vampire.

I only knew one vampire that could help me. The only vampire I'd let live.

The house was quiet and shuttered when I pulled into the driveway. I'd left the engine on, so he'd know I was coming, but maybe he wasn't even at home. I was feeling too frail to hope for anything more than walking out again with my dignity intact.

I walked right up to the front door. Or rather, limped up to the front door. My legs were fine but I kept feeling like I wanted to double over my ribs, like that would ease the uncomfortable pain the bruising caused. I paused at the front door before I rang the bell. I took two deep breaths and winced both times when the expansion of my chest hurt more than when I'd been walking.

I lifted my hand to the doorbell, hovered before I rang it, and finally managed to push it down. Nothing. I wondered if I should ring again. Would that make me impertinent? I was suddenly weak and pathetic. My whole adult life had been about bravado and courage and killing when it was necessary. Doing what was needed to survive. I worked alone and I didn't get attached to anyone or anything. It was bad enough that all of that had been a joke.

It was all pushed to the back now. I didn't have any options anymore. All my arrogance had gotten me a fat lot of nothing. In fact, it had gotten me the opposite of what I'd been doing it for.

It had gotten me angry and frustrated, it had gotten me beaten up. It had gotten Aspen kidnapped.

I rang the bell again and swallowed hard, ignoring the fist of nerves that groped at my gut. I didn't blink an eye when I staked vampires. I was boss with a gun and my leathers. But ringing the doorbell and talking to a man got me in a cold sweat. Bulletproof. Right.

Maybe Joel had been right. I was built backwards.

The thought of him got me to ring the bell a third time. I could stand out here and feel sorry for myself, or I could man up for a change and do the right thing. I was starting to realize 'the right thing' wasn't what I'd always thought it was. In fact, it was the exact opposite.

And I hated that I'd been fooling myself for so long.

"You're going to have to open it yourself and let yourself in," a muffled voice from the other side sounded, yanking me out of my thoughts and kicking me into a new spin of frantic nerves.

"The sunlight is a problem for me." Of course. It was heading on towards late afternoon and the sun was an issue for a purebred. Lately I was getting sloppy, forgetting the facts. I had to pull my act together.

"Can I come in?" I called, certain that when he heard that it was me he would say no. I would barge down the door and demand he see me, I thought.

Yeah right. Me and what army? And in my state? I didn't have any of my vampire killing tools on me, and I didn't want to kill him. Not anymore. He would finally get his wish: I didn't bring my stake.

To be honest I never really did want to kill him.

But I did want to squash him into a corner and get him to help me get Aspen back. It was becoming a desperate nagging at the back of my mind. The hard thoughts, the toughness that I was imagining, made me feel more like myself. Bruised and banged up, yes. But on a mission, and I was never really a woman to take no for an answer.

When he answered 'yes' to my question it threw me off guard. I'd expected a struggle to get into the house.

I opened the door. The house inside was dark and warm, almost humid. I wondered if he'd had heaters on. And I wondered why. I closed the door behind me and the only bit of light that had bled into the black disappeared.

I stood still for a couple of counts, just getting used to the darkness. I could see well enough in the night, provided my eyes were accustomed to the dark.

"What do you want?" Connor's voice flowed around me, deep and caressing like when I'd heard it first. It was that melody that I never wanted to stop listening to. My eyes were getting used to the dark and I still couldn't see him. It was darker deeper into the house. So dark that the blackness was complete. No amount of night vision could let you see something when there was just nothing to see.

I had no idea where he was.

But I could smell him. It was the same smell I'd smelled in the alley that morning when I'd dragged him out of the pending dawn. It was the smell that had surrounded me the first time I'd come here to take him out. The smell that had surrendered me to him when I'd had nothing left but the raw side of me.

It drew me to him just like it had before, a magnetic pull that I'd never felt from any vampire, no matter how pure or how old they'd been when I'd encountered them. And they hadn't been very old, I'd started to realize.

I also knew that Connor was much younger than most vampires I'd met, but he had that thing about him.

"I asked why you're here," he said again because I hadn't answered him. I'd been getting lost in his smell instead. But here it was. The moment of truth; the moment where I was going to have to lay down the courage and bravery I'd managed to scrape together, the arrogance and pride that laced everything I did.

"I need your help," I said. The words scraped my throat as I spoke them and they hung in the air after they'd left my mouth.

"And why should I help you?" he asked. His voice was harsh and I physically flinched. Why indeed?

"There is no reason why you should," I admitted. I was already doing the groveling thing. I might as well lay it on thick if it meant he would help. If it meant we could get Aspen back.

If it meant he would think of me as something worthy again.

"I don't understand you," he said. "The one moment you're kissing me, the next you're killing me, and you never seem very sorry about either."

"I was," I said quickly. "About the killing, I mean. I regret it." I regretted the kissing too, but not for the same reason. I regretted shooting him because I'd been pushed into something I hadn't wanted to do at that point. I'd been scared. Scratch that – I'd been terrified. It wasn't every day that love could kill, but the once in my life that it did, it made me skeptical about love in general. My parents weren't the best example of a healthy relationship.

I regretted kissing him because I'd let myself get emotionally involved with a mark. I'd let myself go. I'd been weak. I'd dared to love again, and I was scared that with that weakness I'd never be able to save Aspen again.

And look where it had gotten me? But I couldn't just keep doing this. I had to fix it. Otherwise I would kill myself, and guilt and shame was a hell of a lot slower than a bullet or a stake.

"I don't think I want to play this game anymore," Connor said and his voice was cold enough to drain the warmth in the room. Maybe the warmth hadn't been from a heater. Maybe it had been him, his emotions. Something.

"Please..." I started but I didn't know what to say. Besides, I was begging. And I hated begging.

"Dammit Adele—"Connor started, flipping on a light switch. The fluorescent light following the click flooded the room, lifting all the colors out and setting them in stark contrast to each other. Harsh, not like light should be. I winced, the sudden light hurting my eyes and by definition my concussed head. But Conner didn't wince or cover his eyes like he had before.

He stared at my face, and all the traces of hostility drained out of his eyes.

"Oh my god," he whispered, letting his eyes roam over my bruises and the way I was trying to hold myself up. "Who did this to you?"

"Please help me get Aspen back," I asked again. "I can't do this alone. You know them well enough to tell me what to expect."

Connor took a step closer to me and I felt my knees wobble. I didn't have the strength to stay upright for long if he was going to come closer to me. He already had me weak at the knees and pathetically head over heels for him. I couldn't do his pity on top of it all.

He stepped up until he was right in front of me, the length of his body mirroring mine, but not touching it. I straightened up and took a deep breath, trying to ignore my ribs. Connor lifted his hand to my face like he was going to touch my eye, but he didn't.

"I'm sorry," he said.

I shook my head and wished I hadn't.

"I'm the one that should be sorry," I said. Connor put his arms on my shoulders, tentatively, like I might break. I didn't, but I wondered about that myself. Gently he pulled me closer to him, and for the first time I let him without a fight. There were no guns, no knives, no battle of wills. It was just Connor, the man it turned out I loved, and me, finally leaning against him.

"I'll help you," he said finally, and I felt my body sag with relief. He held on to me, his arms wrapping around my body, and I let him hold me up for a second before I took my own weight again.

"We just need information," I said when I pulled away from him again and looked into his eyes. They were deep blue, like the ocean, and I wanted to drown in them. But there was no time. "Can we meet here?"

"Who's we?"

"My Martial Arts instructor and a colleague. We're going to get her back but I don't know where to start."

"You're taking on the masters with two humans?" he asked, looking at me like I was crazy. I shrugged and felt like cursing because I kept forgetting I couldn't do the body language I usually used. It damn well hurt.

"I don't really think you should go in there alone," Connor said and I didn't appreciate how know-it-all he sounded. But his face softened. "Not if they did this to you. They'll eat you alive."

I didn't think he meant it figuratively. I shivered.

"You can't come, though. They want you dead. What better time to kill you?"

Connor chuckled. "Don't tell me you're trying to look out for me now? You're a walking conflict."

I was. He was right. But I didn't want him to die. So I loved him. So what? That happened to people, didn't it? Well, not to me. Which was why I didn't want to let the one man that was willing to have me, when I showed only an ugly side, die.

"I don't have anyone else to ask. My people are all missing. Or dead." The last words were so heavy I felt like I might crumble under their weight. Connor must have seen something in my face because his eyes changed, got lighter and deeper. Ringed with a dark green where I swore it had been midnight blue a moment ago.

"I don't want you to go alone," he said. "Get them to come here, we'll talk. And tonight after dark we'll head out."

"I won't let you come with us," I said.

"And I won't let you go without me."

I was too tired to argue. If we all died, well, then we were all dead. There was nothing more I could say about that. I pulled my phone out of my pocket and dialed Carl's number. I gave him the address and he promised to be here in half an hour. He would bring Sensei. Phil. I was going to have to get used to calling him that.

I let them in when they arrived while Connor hid somewhere so the sunlight spilling in through the crack in the door couldn't fry him. When the door was shut and everything was drenched in artificial light, he came out. Carl looked like he was irritated. I wasn't the only one that had had issues about being in friendly terms with vampires. But if I could come round, he could too.

"Behave," I said. "He's one of us."

"Don't you mean you're one of them?" he asked and even though his mouth smiled at me like he'd intended for it to be a joke, his eyes didn't laugh along with it. He'd been serious. And I supposed he was right.

Phil looked at Connor with wide eyes. When Connor spoke and Phil caught a glimpse of his fangs he turned a shade whiter. It was one thing to know every trick in the book about fighting when it came down to humans. Getting to know the night world, even if you were just skirting the edges like Phil was doing now, was a whole other ball game. I wondered if he was revising his fighting technique in his mind.

Connor seemed calm even though we could both smell Phil's nervousness.

"He doesn't bite," I said, and Carl snickered at my poor sentence. I had to admit, it was funny. "Well," I added. "He won't bite *you*, anyway."

Connor smiled and Carl chuckled but Phil didn't look like he thought it was funny. I was guessing that until now he'd really just been thinking it was all a fairy tale. Vampires were damn scary when it came down to it. I was just used to it.

"Okay, so what's the plan?" Carl asked.

Chapter 19

When darkness fell we were almost ready to head out. I'd gone home and suited up in my leathers and my guns. I had it all on me. My Smith & Wesson in my shoulder holster, my Glock at my ankle, my knife at my thigh and the SIG behind my back. The only reason I didn't have the Carbine too was because I didn't want to look suspicious. Three guns and a knife was an overkill already. No pun intended.

I still felt like hell, but I would ignore it. If we got through this I would have the rest of my life to survive. If he died I wouldn't feel my aches and pains anyway.

We had a plan. We had people together to execute it. Most of all we had a drive. We had to succeed. *I* had to succeed.

We weren't really much of an army, no matter how much I was trying to convince myself that we were going to beat the odds. Two humans, one of which only really became aware – truly aware – of the supernatural world tonight. Phil knew how to fight, but what could he do in the face of a vampire with red eyes and teeth that spelled out death?

Carl was used to it all but he was a human. He didn't have superhuman strength or blurring speed or premonitions and the ability to smell blood.

Connor was the opposite. He had all that and none of the skills that a vampire slayer needed. On top of that the relationship between us was like cracked glass. Any moment I was sure it would shatter. There was so much that had happened between us, and we were building our survival on a broken base.

I was in between. The best of both worlds, everyone else had agreed, but I didn't feel that way about it. I was the worst of both worlds. A half-breed that rejected the vampire in me and never really completely made the human side work. Two worlds I never really felt like I fit into.

Yep, we were one hell of a team.

Once the darkness of night was complete, the shimmering quality that always hung like a ghost of the sun's rays finally having seeped away, we headed out. Connor was alert and awake, a vampire at its best. Carl and I were wired. Phil was cautious. We got in Phil's car and drove towards town. I left my bike at Connor's house and it was strange not using it. I couldn't remember the last time I'd been in a car. Maybe before, when life had still been normal.

We headed towards The Palace, a tall shiny glass and metal building in the business district. It was where Jennifer's card said her offices were, and where she'd told me Connor's were too.

We headed to The Palace because it was the most likely place they would be. Connor knew that they were still active at night. I wondered how long he'd known it, why he'd never mentioned it to anyone, like the police for instance. When I asked him about it he shrugged.

"It's not always easy to stop the things you know are wrong. I've been trying."

"But the police could have helped," I said.

"Helped lock me up," was the retort and I dropped it. The truth was I still wasn't a hundred percent sure what to think of him. All I knew was that with my track record, which had been sounding worse and worse to me lately, I couldn't cast the first stone.

The building was dark and quiet, a giant in the night, stretching up into the sky where the night swallowed the top of it and I couldn't see it.

"How are we going to get in?" I asked. "Jennifer said I just had to mention her name to the doorman, but with Connor here..." I didn't want to be rude and point out that he was a wanted man but that was how it was.

"Through the front door," Connor said matter-of-factly, ignoring what I was pointing out.

"We can't just walk in," I said.

"Aren't places like these rigged with security cameras?" Carl asked, his hands in his pockets. He looked like we were going on a field trip, not a fight to the death. I shuddered. I hoped that none of this would go that far, but they'd taken Aspen and she was still alive, so it had to be to draw me in.

"I called in a favor," Connor said and nodded in a direction past the building. When I looked a shadow moved. My chest constricted, but then Carlos stepped into the dim light that reached us from the street.

"You two know each other?" I asked.

"We've done business before, from time to time," Connor said, looking at Carlos, who shrugged. I should have guessed that that would have been the case. If the masters used Carlos and the masters used to work with Connor...

The world seemed too small. There were so many things going in in the dark around corners rather than out in broad daylight.

"It's all taken care of," Carlos said to Connor. "But I don't know how much time you'll have before they notice it."

Phil shivered and I knew it wasn't because he was cold.

"Well, come on," Connor said and he led the way. Somehow he'd taken control, and in a way he was leading the party, even though if I said something I knew he would have followed me. It was nice to have someone else take charge for a change. It was strange to be in a group where I didn't have to just have my own back and that was it. There were more people now, people that seemed to somehow care. And they had my back too.

And I had theirs. So help me, if anything happened to them... I shook my head. I had to focus on the positive.

We didn't take the elevator. Instead we took the stairs, and started the climb. Eighty floors. Of course they weren't going to wait for us on the first floor or even the tenth.

"We could have taken the elevator at least up to floor fifty," Carl heaved. I wondered why he wasn't fit enough for this. Didn't he train? He was the one that had enforced Ruben's advice from the start, that I had to make sure to follow a strict training regime and never get out of shape. When I looked at him he must have known what I was thinking, because he just shrugged like it was supposed to be an explanation all by itself.

"Carlos cut all power," Connor said. "The cameras had back-up systems so exactly this couldn't happen. No elevators. If the masters are here they don't need the light anyway, so with a little luck they won't know we've cut everything."

Most of what he said slid by me, but I hovered on the word 'if'. What if they weren't here? What if it was all wrong?

What if Connor was leading me into a trap?

I shook the last question off. I couldn't think like that. The only way we'd be able to do this now was if we trusted each other. Without it we would fail. If I'd been right, well, then we'd all die. It was pretty simple.

It took us a long time to get to the top, and when we finally got there, even I was huffing and puffing, gasping for air. It didn't matter how fit you were, eighty floors were no joke. After I'd caught my breath I realized that the exhaustion outweighed the pain. My head hurt but I could handle it, and my ribs felt a bit better. I touched my eye gingerly, felt I could open it more. Vampire healing at its best.

The floor was dark. Connor walked first because he could see better than any of us and he knew his offices. Carl followed and Phil after him, and I brought up the rear. The floors were all dark shiny tiles that reflected what little light fell in through the bare windows from the moon. We moved through double doors into a lobby with secretary desks. They were empty. Connor kept moving, turning his head, listening. I strained my ears but I couldn't hear anything. I breathed in deep. Someone was here. I could tell, feel the lifeblood pumping through veins. But I didn't know who it was.

Connor held up his hand and we all froze. Phil looked like he was going to attack the first shadow that moved.

Connor stepped forward and opened the double doors in front of him. I was nervous. If they were there he would die. I hadn't wanted him to come. I hadn't wanted him to lead the team. I hadn't wanted any of this.

And I hadn't had a choice.

Connor poked his head through the door and looked around. I expected all hell to break loose, but there was nothing. A moment later Connor waved us on and he stepped into the room.

When I entered I realized this was what must have been Connor's office. The walls were covered with frames with pictures of Connor as a human, and Jennifer, in some of them. Others were diplomas and degrees in various stuff, and awards he'd been given.

His desk was heavy and dark, with an expensive computer to the one said and stationary scattered across the desk. Connor walked to the desk and slid his hand along the edge of the desk. He missed it. I could tell.

I took a deep breath and picked up a faint smell, something that smelled like it had been burning at some point. With that was anger and fear. And hopelessness.

"Someone's here," I said.

Carl and Phil looked at me, but Connor nodded.

"You're right."

We walked around, following our noses, while the two humans looked on. Phil looked nervous. Carl looked bored.

"In here," Connor said when he got to the door that led to his closet. I glanced at him, my heart suddenly beating in my throat.

Whoever was behind this door could either be an answer or an ending. I took a deep breath and Connor pushed open the door.

Joel lay on the floor, tied up and gagged.

"Joel," I breathed and kneeled beside him. His eyes were closed and his pulse was faint, but it was there. The burning smell was strong now, and his closed were singed. His face was bruised but the bruises weren't new. When I lifted him up and held his head I felt dry blood caked in his hair. This could have been the source of the blood in the pit.

"Joel," I said again, wishing he would answer me.

"It's alright, Adele," Connor said next to me. He's going to be fine."

I trusted him because I didn't know and I desperately had to hold onto something. Joel was alive. I'd expected the worst for so long I felt like I was going to fall over.

"Your techy?" Carl asked. He and Phil both had their heads poked into the closet. I nodded but Connor snapped at them.

"Watch the office, dammit," he said. "If anyone catches us now we're dead."

Phil whipped around and scanned the room but Carl scowled. Connor lifted Joel and he moaned, eyes fluttering open.

"Hey," I said, running my hand down Joel's cheek. His eyes looked like they didn't register anything, staring into a void, but then they slid to me.

"Adele?" he asked with a hoarse voice.

"You're going to be fine," I said and my voice was thick. I scolded myself, commanding myself not to cry. "We're going to get you to a hospital."

Connor managed to get Joel out of the office.

"Can we get him to a hospital?" I asked Connor.

"We have to," he agreed. "And then where are we headed?"

I stood up and stretched myself out. The bruises on my body were feeling better and better. I looked around the office, feeling forlorn. There was no one else here. Joel had been alone. It made me feel like I'd failed. Again.

"She's not here," I said, feeling the void open in my chest as I said it. Where was I supposed to find her now?

"We'll just have to move on, then," Connor said.

"Where?"

We all fell quiet because the fact was that none of us knew the answer to that.

"I don't know," Connor said softly. I paced in a circle in front of the hospital. The bright lights streaming from the emergency rooms lit up the pavement around me as bright as daylight. It made my black leather clothes look blacker. Connor looked ghostly white in the light, like a marble statue.

I closed my eyes and reached out for her. It took me a while to reach out into the night, to still my insides. When my heart rate was slowed right down and I could almost track the molecules in my body I was concentrating that hard, I picked up the faint hum in my veins that didn't come from my blood, but Aspen's. It was fading. I took a deep breath, trying to ignore my stomach that felt like stone. When I breathed it felt like my throat was only half the size, hard with panic.

I opened my eyes. "I can't find her," I said. The panic crept into my voice.

"What do you mean?" Carl asked. Connor understood. He looked at me, his eyes asking me questions. I nodded. I had her blood in my veins, however little. But it wasn't enough.

"They keep shutting me out. I can't find her," I said. "I know she's alive, but I don't know where she is. It's like she's behind a metal wall."

"She might very well be," Connor said. Phil and Carl both looked like they didn't know what I was talking about, like they were missing something.

"What do you mean?" I asked.

"If they have her they might stop her from being able to dematerialize."

"She can't do that," I said. "She only has half of the genes, like me. Or wouldn't they know that? She looks more vampire than I do."

Connor shook his head. "I doubt they don't know. But they might keep her where they've kept other vampires before. Vampires that can dematerialize."

What he was saying took two seconds to sink in before I understood. They might have been keeping her in the same place where they kept the other vampires. The one they sold. My hand raised to my mouth involuntarily.

"How are we going to find her?" I asked. I was getting frantic. After all this, what if we were too late after all? What if we never found her? What if she died before I got to her? What if...?

"Don't do this," Connor said, putting his hands on my wrists, pulling my hands away from my face. I hadn't realized I'd buried myself in the palms of my hands. When my fingers came away from my face they were trembling.

"Don't do it," he said again. His voice was soft, gentle. "They're doing this because they are vampires. Because they can. You can do it, too. Just find her. Focus, and find her."

"But I'm only half, Connor. I'm not—"

"You can do it," he said. "You can. I believe in you."

Chapter 20

I glanced at Phil. He shrugged. Carl looked bored. Somewhere along the lines we'd lost both of them – they didn't understand what was going on. I took a deep breath. Connor was right. This was all I had left. And I hated it.

"Are we going to get a move on?" Carl asked, sounding a lot less bored than he looked.

"We just need to find her, "Connor said in a calm voice, not taking his eyes off me.

"How?" Phil asked. Connor just shook his head, eyes glued to mine. Carl finally seemed to understand. For someone who'd been hunting vampires for so long it took him a long time to catch up.

"I think Adele can trace her blood," he explained.

"Like a tracker?"

"Something like that."

Phil looked horrified. Maybe he'd put two and two together after all. I ignored him, ignored both of them. Phil had wanted to come along, he'd agreed. This was the night world. This was what I was, somewhere deep down inside. If he didn't like it no one was forcing him to stay. But he didn't leave.

I took a deep breath and blew it out with a shudder. I hadn't done this, ever. I had rejected this side of me since the days I was signed up for therapy. Since I'd been placed with a foster family that were human. I closed my eyes, and calmed myself again. I imagined this was what it was like to dematerialize. I focused on myself, my body. The beat of my heart, pumping blood through my veins. They movement of the platelets that carried oxygen. The rise and fall of my chest as I breathed in and out. Slowly I found Aspen's pulse, dimly fluttering next to my own. It was weak because of the little blood I had in me that belonged to her. Not because she was fighting for her life. I realized that now.

Maybe if I were a vampire I would have dematerialized now. I felt like I was made of a stone the same way vampires looked when they had time to think about disappearing.

And there it was again. The metal wall that slammed into place, blocking me from finding Aspen. I knew she was alive. I still felt the echo of her heartbeat in my veins. But I couldn't find her. It was like a GPS searching for signal.

I willed it away with my mind. With everything I had inside me. I reached deep down, to the person I'd pushed away for so long I almost didn't know who she was again. The person that could feel further and deeper than a human, or even a half breed. The person that was stronger, and faster, and more elegant. A creature of the night.

I dug deep down, and found the vampire.

I pushed back against the metal wall, forced my whole will against it. It wouldn't budge at first. But then, slowly, it started to move, almost like I was pushing it. I threw everything I had into it, and finally it gave way faster and faster, until I could feel her again. Almost see her in my mind's eye. Just a silhouette, but her wavy hair moved in a breeze and her fingers curled around the arms of her wheelchair. I could feel the despair, the fear, the panic.

It felt like I was peeling away from the world I knew. My head started pounding and I felt dizzy. And suddenly I knew where she was.

When I opened my eyes all three men were staring at me. Carl looked amused. Phil looked shocked. And Connor looked at me with so much emotion in his eyes I was scared he would choke on it.

"Caldwell Street," I said and my voice sounded different. "The house in Caldwell Street. That's where she is."

When I spoke something nicked my lip and a sharp pain shot into it.

"Ow," I said, and when I licked it I tasted blood. I frowned, bringing a finger to my lip, and then to my teeth. I had vampire teeth, pointed, needle tips. When I pulled my finger away it was red with blood, and it tasted metallic in my mouth.

"Well," Connor said, and in that word he held the whole world.

"Well," I answered, because I'd finally found myself. I'd finally come home.

Connor frowned, the words I'd spoken finally dawning on him. "Caldwell Street?" he asked. "But I got rid of that."

"You owned it?" Carl asked.

"I lived there until the change. I sold it so that I could disappear."

"Who did you sell it to?" I asked.

"I don't know."

"I do," I said.

We drove up the hill in silence. There wasn't a lot to be said. We were heading right to the lair, the midpoint of everything. This new truth, this new person, the one I really was, was all a bit new for me, and I felt foreign in my own skin.

"What will we do when we get there?" Phil asked. That was a fair question.

"I think you should stay in the car," I said to Phil. He wasn't trained in any of the vampire-killing art, and even Carl and I, who'd been doing this for a long time, were outmatched. These vampires were a lot stronger.

"I agree with Adele," Connor said, but when I looked at Phil he didn't look like he was upset with the arrangement. He'd been noble, and in any other fight I'd want him at my back. But this time he was in over his head. It had been a mistake to bring him.

The three of us peeled out of the car and walked the last couple of yards to the gate. We stopped in front of it, the brown rustic metal gate reaching far above our heads.

"How do we get in?" Carl asked. He was already pacing along the wall, trying to see if there was a way in, but I knew that there would be no way in.

"We can go in through the servant's entrance," Connor said. "I doubt they kept the codes the same for the main gate, but the servants have their own gate and their own code."

"And if that's changed?" I asked.

"Well, then we'll think of a plan B."

Connor turned and followed the wall that reached far up above us. Carl and I followed. Connor made it way to the end of the wall where I thought the next property started, but I realized the wall dipped in and a narrow passage led between the two properties. I felt claustrophobic with tall walls on both sides and very little space to move other than forward or back. Connor was in front of me, Carl behind me, and somehow that didn't make me feel much better. The whole place had a foreboding feeling to it, like something was waiting to go wrong any second.

Connor finally reached a door made of the same rustic metal as the main gate. It was arched and narrow like the rest of the passage. Connor took out a key and turned it. He might have been able to materialize inside, but neither of us could.

"What if they have cameras?" Carl asked.

"Then they see us," Connor answered. "We're going to have to face them sooner or later."

Carl nodded but he looked like he'd rather turn back and wait for Phil. He swallowed hard and Conner pushed open the door. It was like magic. We followed him through it into the garden, and he closed the door behind us. I didn't want it closed, but keeping it open would show whoever found it that something was wrong.

The garden was huge, with big trees scattered across a perfectly manicured law. The moon cast a silver light on everything, and the garden looked like it belong in a fairy tale. We followed the shadows, sticking to them as much as we could. A long winding drive way ran through the garden, with cobbles that had an Italian feel to them, and a big fountain decorated a circle at the front door where cars could drive around to head back to the gate. Garages were lined up on the other side of the property.

Connor beckoned us in the opposite direction. We crept silently up the stair that led to the balcony on the first floor, and it was only a miracle we hadn't been seen yet. Either they were waiting for us because they knew we were coming, or we were managing to slip through. I was hoping it was the latter.

The house was incredible. In any other circumstance I would have admired it, envied it. Wanted it. I wasn't one for living in the lap of luxury, but this wasn't just money. It was art. I was impressed with Connor's taste.

He led us through a maze of passages and rooms until we finally found a room where he stopped.

"There's metal in these walls," he said in a whisper. I tried to access the new part of me that I'd only found earlier, and after struggling a few seconds I found it, and I could feel it too. It felt the same way it felt when my mind was foggy and I couldn't quite remember what I wanted to say. If they were anywhere, it would be in there.

Suddenly a scream echoed through the house, so loud it vibrated in my bones long after it stopped.

"What was that?" Carl asked.

"Celia," I answered. This was it. I turned, and she appeared as if out of nowhere in front of me.

"Adele," Connor started but I waved him off.

"Let me deal with this. Keep Carl safe. She's mine."

The words were barely out of my mouth when she attacked with a hiss. I hissed too, and launched for her. When he collided it was like an explosion. She had her claws out and scratched at me. I was faster now, stronger, and I couldn't believe I hadn't made an effort to accept myself earlier. She noticed the change, and her movements became careful.

I managed to out-maneuver her, and I sunk my teeth into her arm. She screamed and a shudder rippled through her body. When I let go her arm bled onto the floor. I could smell her blood, warm and sweet, different, supernatural. The same scent of flowers hung in the air.

"You've acquired some skills," she said, clutching her bleeding arm against her body.

"Never show your enemy everything you can do right away," I said. Of course this wasn't true. If I'd been able to do this before I would have taken her out the first time. But it sounded great when I said it and the scowl on her face was worth it.

She jumped at me again. I ducked, but she upped her game too, knowing what I was capable of now, and her nails scraped down my cheek and neck. I hissed at her and felt my skin. It was ripped and sticky with blood. I curled my lips back in a snarl, but the feeling in my neck and my face stopped me in my tracks. I was healing fast, I could feel it close up. Celia couldn't do that. I grinned, smug.

She knew it too. This was it. This was the fight. She wasn't going to toy with me like a cat with a mouse anymore. If she didn't give it everything she wouldn't make it.

I wasn't planning for that to happen anyway.

I jumped at her first. She'd been stunned, watching the wound on my face heal in front of her, and she'd been caught off guard. I grabbed a handful of hair and yanked, hard. She moaned and rolled me over, getting in a hit that would have been a problem if I still had the concussion she'd left me with.

But I was fine, and besides stunning me for just a second, it did nothing.

I braced myself and threw everything I had into it, throwing her off me. I landed on her, pushing her elbows down with both knees. Her eyes were pools of black, surrounded by green. I could feel her tentacles reach into my mind, by I closed it and pushed her out. Her eyes widened.

"Please, don't—"she started but I cut her off. I pushed my silver stake in under her ribs and angled it upward. I pushed in deeper, finding her heart, and her pulse throbbed and then stopped. Her eyes were wide, mouth frozen in a silent 'o' before her features went slack and she collapsed.

"Remind me not to get on your bad side," Carl said behind me. When I got off Celia and turned he was looking at me like I was a goddess and he hadn't known it before.

"We had a history," I said.

"I can see that."

When I looked at Connor he smiled. I didn't think it was because of my lack of feeling when I murdered Celia. I thought that maybe it was because of who I'd become. I smiled and I felt my own teeth on my lips. It was a strange sensation, but not altogether unfamiliar. I wondered at which point I'd forgotten I'd always had them as a child.

"We have to get in there," Connor said, nodding towards the door.

I took a deep breath. It didn't matter how in touch I was with myself. These guys were still the master vampires that had killed Zelda and Ruben. Carl swallowed hard enough for me to hear next to me, and I knew he thought the same thing.

"Together," I said to him, and he understood. A part of this would be for Ruben after all.

Connor felt the door but it was locked. Somehow I hadn't thought it would be open. There was no way to get in, I could feel the metal all round. So Connor knocked on the door like we had an appointment. Sometimes the only way to go was forward.

For a moment nothing happened. Then the door clicked like a lock was being turned, and it opened.

The leader opened the door.

"Well," he said, looking at Connor and then at me. "We knew she'd eventually arrive, but we didn't expect you."

"Vladimir," Connor said as a greeting. Well, if there was ever a scary vampire with a scary name, this was it. The vampire smiled with teeth that still seemed horrible, even I had a set of my own now, and his eyes flashed red. He didn't look friendly at all.

"Come, come in," he said. "We have everything ready for you."

He stepped aside and we walked into the room. I was last to go in, and as soon I was through the door I found a wall and put my back to it so I faced the entire room. I had guns and knives on me, but somehow it didn't feel like it was enough. These vampires weren't here to play games.

I didn't know what I'd expected, but the room, besides the menacing vampires in it, was very normal. Rich, but normal. It was carpeted from wall to wall with a thick white carpet that I sank into. The walls were painted a wine red, and the furniture was all black. Leather couches formed a cozy half-circle around an unlit fireplace, a lacquered desk stood in a corner with stacks of papers and files, and the back wall was covered with ceiling-height bookshelves with leather bound books. The other vampires, number two, I decided, lounged on a leather sofa.

I noticed there were two big windows with black curtains drawn across from me. The material looked like it was leaded, heavy, dragging down. The same as the covers they put over women in x-ray machines. They could keep light out all by themselves.

There were no other vampires in the room. I had thought maybe there would be hostages. But there was no one.

Vladimir walked to the wall and pushed a button, and a bar rolled out. Fancy.

"Can I offer you anything to drink?" he asked. We all shook our heads. He shrugged and picked up a wine glass, taking a sip. The wine was a dark red, and thick. I frowned, and then the smell reached me. It wasn't wine at all, it was blood.

I gasped for me breath about the same time Connor did. Vladimir laughed.

"Not so tough after all, the two of you," he said in a voice that suddenly sounded deeper, harder. He pointed a long finger at Carl. "Only he seems to have the stomach for this. But he's just a human. I doubt he knows what this is."

I felt suddenly nauseous.

"Where's Aspen?" I asked, hoping my voice sounded more confident than I felt. "I'm here for my sister."

"Yes, I thought so. Of course, killing him would have been fine. But I see you brought him here. Did you hope we would do it for you?"

He was talking about Connor. Carl stepped in front of Connor, and Vlad and his number two laughed.

"There's a fine line between bravery and stupidity," he said. He moved so fast I hadn't even seen him move. Not even a blur. The one moment he'd been by the bar, the next he had Carl pinned against the wall, the blood in his glass still dancing from side to side.

"Don't!" I called out. Vladimir smiled with a terrible smile, one that promised bloodshed.

"He's done nothing to deserve dying," I said.

"And still you brought him."

"I volunteered," Carl said but his throat was squeezed shut so the words came out as a wheeze. He was going to get himself killed.

"Are you going to beg for mercy like your boss?" Vladimir asked Carl, squeezing tighter. Carl squirmed in his hand, legs kicking, hands groping at the fingers around his neck. His face went red.

I pulled out a gun and aimed it at Vladimir's head. The Smith & Wesson would take his head off.

"I'll shoot," I said. "Let him go."

Vladimir looked at me, his eyes turning from amused to menacing.

"You threaten me? You're an abomination and you have the arrogance to stand there and point a gun at me? For you that you'll—"

Carl had kicked him between the legs. It didn't matter who you were, vampire or not, a kick to the balls hurt like hell. He didn't double over or gasp for breath or drop to the ground like a human. But he did drop Carl, and it bought me time. Carl gasped for air and scrambled across the floor to me. If he could get under my gun I could cover him.

Vladimir growled like an animal and grabbed Carl's ankle, ripping him up and flinging him across the room. I heard bones snap and Carl cried out. He hit the far wall, and then he sunk to the floor, unconscious. He was out of the way, badly hurt, but not dead. Not yet.

Vladimir turned to me.

"The girl," he barked and number two moved. Another door opened, and they wheeled Aspen out. She looked frail and vulnerable, hanging in her chair. Her arms were strapped to her chair so she couldn't wheel herself and her head was bowed, her blond hair a curtain.

When I gasped she looked up, and when she saw me, she stilled.

"Adele?" she said and her voice was tiny. But she looked okay, not even harmed.

"We're going to get you out of here, angel," I said. She smiled and nodded. She believed me. And I would.

"You can let us go now," I said. "We'll be taking my sister and leaving."

The two vampires looked at each other, smiled, and then burst out laughing like I'd made a joke.

"Really, Adele," Vladimir said. He looked into my eyes, and suddenly the world went black.

When I opened my eyes again, hours had passed. I could feel it. I looked around me. I lay on the floor, unable to move. Connor lay by the curtains, eyes closed. Carl was bent at a bad angle, still unconscious. Aspen sat across from me, looking exhausted and worried. When she saw me awake, her face changed, relief, but she didn't make a sound. Smart.

The vampires were talking together in hushed tones and I couldn't hear them.

Vladimir turned to me, suddenly aware that I was awake.

"You're not as strong as we thought you were, after killing Celia."

She couldn't have been much loved if they didn't care she was dead.

"Didn't you at least like her?" I asked. My mouth worked fine even though I couldn't move anything else.

Vladimir shrugged. "She didn't do her job well enough. Death is a fair motivation for that. She lost."

I tried to move again, but I couldn't.

"What are you going to do?" I asked.

"We're going to wait for sunrise," Vlad said, looking at his watch. And then we're going to leave, and those curtains are going to open. And you're going to watch Connor die in the first rays of dawn."

That was cruel. Inhumane.

"You can't do that," I said.

Vladimir walked over to me and I could feel the vibrations of his weight on the floor underneath the carpet as he came closer to me. He kneeled in front of me and grabbed my chin. It hurt. He tipped my head and looked at my fangs, frowning. Probably trying to remember if they'd been there before. Then he yanked my head to the side and my head throbbed, my chin aching.

"Oh, but we can," he said.

"Master," number two called. He'd sat down at a laptop and he pointed to the screen. Vladimir walked toward the desk and looked at the screen. He swore.

"Fix it," he said.

Number two typed furiously, but he looked panicked. Maybe his punishment for failure would be death too.

"Business deal gone wrong?" I asked innocently. Both vampires scowled and I knew I'd hit a nerve. The time was ticking on, and I realized it was sunrise. They could still kill Connor with it, but they wouldn't have their dramatic death. They were still fighting about whatever was happening on their screen. I managed to slide my eyes to Aspen. She sat quietly, looking at me, and I wondered what she was thinking. She was scared, it hung in the air, coming off her skin, but it was old, like she'd been feeling it too long for it to be full strength. Her arms were taped to the wheelchair and with how frail she was I knew she couldn't break free of them. If only someone could open those damn curtains.

I fought against whatever spell was holding me down, but no matter how hard I struggled I couldn't move. I closed my eyes and focused, but even my vampire abilities I'd only come in contact with recently weren't good enough. The fact was that they were older and stronger than me.

I groaned inwardly. When I looked at Connor, his eyes were finally open. He looked at me, and his eyes were big and blue, resigned. He knew they were going to kill him. He knew as well as I knew. And he wasn't scared. He was angry.

All this, and this was how it ended?

The door flung open, and something shot past me. It was Phil. The vampires both hissed and moved to him, but he had caught them by surprise. He'd yanked the curtains away from the window. It had only opened a crack, but one line of sunlight was enough. Vladimir froze halfway on his way to Phil, and screamed. Then he burst into ash and fell to the floor in a cloud of dust.

Number two hissed and drew to the further corner. He was sizzling and smoking but it wasn't direct light. With Vladimir dead I could suddenly move again. I rolled over and drew my Smith & Wesson. I didn't take the time to aim properly. I just fired.

Number two looked down at his chest. Blood oozed out of it from a hole as big as an eye. I'd hit the heart, and it had been with silver. It didn't matter how well he healed, it was over for him. He looked at me, his face blank, and then he fell to the floor. My arm was numb from the recoil, and I lowered my hand to the floor, lying there for a second. Then I pushed myself up.

Connor, also able to move again, was curled against another wall, moaning and smoking as well. I jumped up and yanked the curtain closed again, and the complaint stop. Phil sat huddled in a ball at my feet.

"They're dead," I said, tapping Phil on the shoulder.

"Thank god," he said and stood up.

"No, thank you," I said and gave him a hug. "If it weren't for you we'd be lost."

He smiled. I turned to Aspen and cut her tape with my knife. Her eyes were squeezed shut.

"It's okay, Aspen," I said, kneeling in front of her. "It's over."

"I knew you'd come for me," she said.

"Of course."

She took a deep breath and looked at me like she was seeing me for the first time.

"You look different."

I looked at my leathers and shrugged. "I didn't really want you to see me like this." But she shook her head.

"I don't mean your clothes and your guns. I mean you. Your teeth. And... well, just you."

I smiled, and she smiled back.

"I'm going to have nightmares about this for weeks," she said, nodding toward number two on the floor in a pool of blood that colored the carpet a dark red.

"I'm sorry," I said, and I hugged her.

When I got up, Phil was bent over Carl.

"I think he needs help," he said. He pulled out his phone and called 911. Connor walked to me and he looked like he had bad sunburn.

"You look like shit," I said. He grinned.

"You look amazing," he said, and I felt myself flush. And then I realized that for the first time in a very long time, I felt it.

Chapter 21

Everything was different after that. Aspen and I found a place where we could stay together for a while until I could make arrangements for a new live in nurse. She didn't want anyone just yet. She'd been close to Zelda, and her death had been painful.

She got nightmares for a long time. She'd seen Zelda get killed and we never found Claude. After a year the police suggested we expect the worst. It didn't go down well.

Joel recovered and he went back to working for a company that did their job during daylight hours. He had some pirating business on the side for a thrill, but I had the idea he was done with the night world for a while. He was sweet on my sister, and the way she lit up for him was enough for me not to take his head off for dating her. She deserved a guy, and if anyone was a good guy, it was Joel. It wasn't very serious yet, but it would be. I could feel it.

Carl had a leg broken in three places, two broken ribs and a hell of a concussion, but he made it out alive, and we stayed friends. He came over every now and then and we pretended to be friends even though we didn't always get along. What he did for a living was a mystery, he never told us, but I had a feeling we'd all had enough of the darkness. He didn't like to admit that he owed his life to a martial arts instructor that he didn't like so we didn't talk about it. Neither of us knew what had happened to Sonya but Ruben's company closed and a nightclub opened in its place. I would never go there again.

I didn't go back to the ugly side of the world. It had been hard enough as it was. Instead I'd managed to find a job at the Academy, training with Phil, teaching classes of my own in self-defense, fighting techniques, and we were thinking of branching out to a shooting range. I spent every day with Phil, knowing that if it hadn't been for the most inexperienced, most human one of us all, we'd all be dead.

Connor and I had visited my father a week after the incident.

"Who's this?" he'd asked when Connor had sat next to me. I'd looked at Connor, and he'd smiled, his blue eyes encouraging me to face my past and deal with it.

"He's my boyfriend," I'd said. "I love him."

My dad had nodded.

"Why are you here?" he'd asked the way he always did.

"I came to say..." I took a deep breath. "I forgive you."

My father's face crumpled and he pinched the bridge of his nose with his thumb and forefinger.

"And goodbye," I added. This was the last time. When he'd looked up at me again, he'd nodded.

I'd gotten up, and Connor and I had walked out into the night, hand in hand.

"Did you mean it?" he'd asked.

"Someday, I'll come to mean it," I said. "But for now, it was right to say it."

We'd walked into the night, world that accepted me now, that didn't hold monsters and hell wherever I looked.

Jennifer disappeared. It was in the news. Either she left the country, or she turned. I guessed we would never find out.

And me? I didn't know who I was just yet, but I would find out. With Aspen and Joel, Connor and Phil, and Carl we made a twisted but fairly happy family. And we accepted each other for what we were, and what we weren't. They only thing I wasn't willing to give up yet was my bike.

I may not have been a vampire slayer anymore, but I was still Adele Griffin. I liked my bike and my guns and my leathers, and everyone loved me for it, me included.

And those who didn't, could suck it.

Check my next book in the Series! <u>*Vampire's Shade 2*</u>
Or
*Get even better value for money when you purchase
the Vampire's Shade Discounted Box Set for $7.99, instead of
paying a total of $12 when you buy each book separately.
Just type* "**Vampire's Shade Discounted Box Set**" *on the Store
Search Bar.*

<u>*Get our 'next releases' notification*</u>
*Leaving a customer review would help other readers, and
will take just a minute of your time*

Lightning Source UK Ltd.
Milton Keynes UK
UKOW02f2032201116
288138UK00001B/9/P